RAIN

RAIN

Kirsty Gunn

Atlantic Monthly Press
New York

First published in Great Britain in 1994 by Faber and Faber Limited
First Atlantic Monthly Press edition, April 1995

Printed in the United States of America

FIRST AMERICAN EDITION

Library of Congress Cataloging-in-Publication Data

Gunn, Kirsty
     Rain / Kirsty Gunn.
     ISBN 0-87113-592-2
     I. Title.
  PS3557.U4864R35 1995   813'.54—dc20   94-44375

The Atlantic Monthly Press
841 Broadway
New York, NY 10003

10 9 8 7 6 5 4 3 2 1

For David

UP IN THAT PART the water smelled rivery. We hadn't even passed the little bay at the end of the first beach but already the air was touched by the promise of our destination. All the trees were drowning. They reached their long skinny branches into the lake, leaning so far that their gnarled roots could barely hold the clay. You knew it was only time before whole bodies would be dislodged, allowed to drift, then sink. The water would seal over them again and that's how it would end: you would never know there had been trees there at all.

There was a glut of water at the lake, miles and miles of freshwater wash spread over the curve of the earth with no horizon of land you could see. Still the rivers and streams ran into it, still-melting snow off the mountains sluiced the blue channels dark with cold. Every year the water-levels rose. Water crept up higher and higher on the sand, another lump of earth was crumbled away. Even on the road you could see signs of its advance: pumice crumbled in the gutters, green weed stains on the tarmac from where the lake had flooded in spring. It came from building on a land spit, people said. You couldn't claim it gave you real foundations.

As the beach curved away from the few pale, wooden houses that marked our summer town it disappeared. If you wanted to walk that way, past the drowned bay and beyond, you had to wade and then climb up onto the grass, pushing through the thick clusters of lupins that grew there. Your hands parted the tough yellow blooms that closed again behind you like a seam, the warp and weft of heads and stalks unbroken. It wasn't until you came over the other side of the rise that the growth thinned out, back to scraggy grass again, frilled at the edges with sand.

Further on, past the bushes and up and over the rocky hump at the end of the first beach, the sand swept wide again. Low cloud came in over the lake in the mornings and in the pale, thick light the water, lapping on the white shore, was like cream. Swimming out into it you could feel how, with each stroke, you were further and further into whiteness, folding into the air like an angel.

'Don't go!' I heard Jim crying, far away. 'Come back to where I am, it's scary there.'

Strange, he believed I would leave him when he was the one who was always trying to get away. He ran from me as soon as we reached the second beach, springing ahead onto the wide tablet of sand like a little dog let off a lead. He ran in great sweeping circles, around and around, backwards and forwards from the water to the dry.

'I'm over here! Look at me!'

My elastic boy.

What was the need in him that carried him from me yet kept him to be within my sight? Later I found out that lovers did this, had the instinct to be solitary while wanting glances, touches to ensnare them. Was he like one of those? A trained creature who could swoop away yet was retained by an invisible thread? What was it that took him out, brought him back, took him out again and left him? His voice looped now, lightly over the quiet air, floated.

'Hey . . .' he called. 'Watch this . . .'

Over at the edge of the lake he was throwing tufts of pumicey sand into the water.

'Take that!' he flung another handful, and another. 'Take that! And that!'

The sand sprinkled like sugar on the surface. He watched it for a minute, delicate, then was off again, spinning along the moistened rim of the beach, picking up a stick and dragging it behind him, leaving a mark that dissolved as fast as it was made, then dropping it and running off again, released further and further into distance until he was just a seed.

He was my younger brother by seven years. James Edward, born 1967. Jim Little, my mother called him. 'Because I'll never let you grow . . .'

She had lots of special names for people, she jingled them around until they became habit. 'You can be Petal Pie or Sweetie,' she said to me. 'But don't forget your Daddy's always "My Boyfriend" . . .'

3

On the days when she stayed in her darkened room, when she was sick or resting, she didn't use the private names. It was more a thing for parties or a cheerful mood – putting her make-up on as she dressed for the evening, or chasing my little brother fresh out of his bath, wearing her yellow bikini.

'Come here my little fishy tadpole, I want you for my supper!'

He slipped away from her and ran out the door, naked and shining.

'You can't catch me . . .' He danced around on the buffalo grass that grew outside the house, the lake tilting golden behind him as the sun went down.

'Put on your pyjamas and come to bed, Jim Littlefish.' My mother held out a blue towel to trap him. 'Come in now or I'll cuddle you to death . . .'

Our parents had parties all summer, they started at dusk and went on deep into the hot night. The lights were on in every room, spilling out onto the lawn, and the music from the record-player was turned up loud.

Love, love me do.
You know I love you.
I'll always be true.
So ple-e-e-ease. Love me do.

The adults loved the songs, they sang along and danced. If you'd walked past our house at night, hearing them, seeing them together in that way, you might have thought: I would like to live there, be pressed up with them against the windows. You might have wished your mother was as beautiful.

The dawn would be ashy with cigarette ends when Jim and I came downstairs in the morning. People were sleeping on the sofas, spilt food around them and the empty sound of a record spinning in its groove. There were bridge parties and cocktail parties, and petrol barbeques when my father charred dripping steaks over a naked, leaping flame. No matter how much the house was cleaned afterwards, the smell of meats always lingered. Sometimes I believed I could smell it on our skin.

For all those summer holidays Jim stayed little, he never seemed to grow. It was like my mother's spell had come true. He remained miniature and perfect, a tiny bird-boy with a tracery of fragile bones and shoulder-blades that stuck out like wings.

'Come on! Hurry up!'

His voice carried across the warm grey air. No urgency was conveyed by it, how could it be?

'Hurry on!'

I was never fast enough for him. I was too much of an older sister, I suppose, walking behind, making perfect footprints in the sand. There was a faded T-shirt I wore that made me feel like a teenager. When I reached him he was sitting down, legs crossed, drifting sand through his fingers. I could have put my arms around his whole body and contained him there, neatly as a parcel. He was tanned dark from the sun, tumbled like a stone to smoothness. But for his soft cotton shorts he was bare.

'Don't do that!' He shook his head away when I wanted to place my hand on his silky hair, feel how warm it was, how it smelled of sunshine and sand and clean water. 'I'm not a girl.'

As we came further along the beach the depth of the lake fell away, receding into distance. At first there were only rivulets and small puddles stranded on the wide sand, ridged patterns of waves left dented in the wet, but as you walked on, getting closer to the river-mouth, you could see that water coated the beach entirely in a thin film. Here was a plate of water, a tray, where you could walk out for miles towards the horizon and still be no deeper than your ankles. Clear fish darted in the shallows like electric currents and if we stood quite still they came right up to us and kissed our feet with tiny fish lips. Nothing bad could happen. There were no hooks to catch or lines to bring you down, no deep ledges or treacherous currents could tug your body away. The sun shone, diffused behind the layers of mist and gauzy cloud, and Jim Little ran out upon the lovely shining skim, sparks of water charging up from his heels in a spray. The grey light opened around him, at my back condensed. The water loved my brother too much.

It was a strange freshwater tide that had slipped over the beach and done this: the river. Twice a day it caused the lake to rise and fall, disgorging water into water when it was full, spreading across the sand when the level was low. From out of the cleft of bush it came on, a slow deep plough of water carving a smooth passage between the hills, wanting to change. As you came closer

6

you saw how dark the water was, how complicated by shadows from the overhanging growth, how the jade insides of the water were flecked with gold. Trapped below the water's surface, hanks of pale blond weed washed endlessly downstream. It was so quiet you could hear the water sucking around the strands, so quiet you could hear bubbles of air forming and breaking, the soaken air trying to breathe.

No one knew how far up the river went or what the country was like in the place where it came from. You could travel upstream for miles, for days, for weeks, my father told me, and still find yourself no closer to the water's source. The river would continue, quiet and knowing, while all the time you went deeper and deeper into the country, the colours of the bank changing from orange to yellow, clay to dun, rocky and wet with leaves in the parts where the sun never got to it. There would be a place where vines would wrap themselves around the rotting tree stumps like terrible old lovers, their ropey arms strangling anything else that tried to grow there. Wild pigs might come and snuffle you out, or a deer would step from the shadows into a clearing, blinking in the light. With every step you would find yourself covered with thick brown dust from the ferns, your skin may be bruised and torn. Perhaps the bush would be cleared, in parts, into scrubby farmland with a few mangy sheep. A dog might have barked outside a hut made of sheets of corrugated iron, rusted red and black, and maybe someone lived there, or maybe they were dead.

I guess a thousand, a thousand thousand rivers must have run into the lake, trickling threads of water, slim deep channels, waterfalls and rocky rapids breaking their surface so violently that watching them would be like watching glass breaking over and over, in thunderous pieces and shards and sprays of white, white powder. Yet, with all those rivers pouring in, adding water to water, charged with fish, thick with twigs and leaves from where they had broken off the hillsides way upstream and drifted down, only our one seemed to have contained within it all the places it had been.

'Let's go and discover . . .' I turned for Jim Little, with his face-mask and damp hair he was meant as a child for rivers, and realized he was gone. Suddenly emptiness was all about me. In the still water, silence; in the carved trees no breath.

'Where are you?' I heard my voice go out into nothing. 'Where are you?' I started to run. Already he was slipping away forever into the second of his leaving. 'Where are you?'

How my awful voice pierced the opaque sky, sent out alone for his returning. 'Where are you?' it cried. 'Where are you?'

The cry came back from the hills empty. 'Where are you?' it echoed, quieter now. 'Where are you?' As if the hills could have saved him. Their massive shoulders rose straight out of the water, the darkness of their reflection cast like a cloak about them. Old mothers, they had no children.

From way off there, out on the thin lake, he heard me,

turned, hesitated for a minute. Then he saw me, started to run.

'Wait for me!'

Behind me the hills rose, the sky was darkening.

'Hurry!' I called. There was no time.

'Wait for me!'

'Hurry!'

'Don't leave me!'

Now he runs towards me and I hold it, that minute. I own it. The silver sheet of water trembles about him as he comes, running back to me through the light air. I cry out – a sound, no words. My youngest, smallest brother . . . For five years he occupied my life, all his movements, his few words, mine. The lovely bend of his fine limbs was the dream I had for my own body, to be light and careless and, with no heaviness of speech and thought, in endless, continuous motion of flight. Even today I think how my brother, running out of the low milky cloud, his cotton shorts a blur of faded red, is me. It lasts a lifetime, that moment of him coming towards me. His whole self, mine, is caught up there in that particular combination of muscle and bone and skin and hair. And how strange it is that, for the complexity of it, for all the gathering up that there was in his running, when he reached me it was as if he had simply stepped out of the air to be by my side.

'Hi,' he said and he took my hand.

There was a jetty near the mouth of the river, not very big, where everyone kept their boats. It was sheltered there. The stilts sank deep into the still green water for strength and even in a high winter wind the boats would be safe, bumping their white and painted sides gently against each other, tucked away from the lake's great expanse. To get to the jetty you had to follow a narrow path that curled from the open beach into the bush. In there, for a few steps, you were surrounded so closely by growth that you could have felt stifled by it, the way it pushed in on you, surrounded you with its dark odours, but then you turned the corner and suddenly you were out by the river again with the wood of the jetty worn smooth under your feet, boats bobbing on either side.

We had a small sailboat tied up there, though nobody used it. Jim and I weren't allowed to take it out on our own and our parents rarely sailed, but my brother and I liked to go and sit in it anyway. Although it was moored to the wooden pole, tied and trapped, the sound of the water slapping against its sides was enough. If you faced out towards the river you didn't see the other boats moored on either side and it was like you were the only ones on the water, alone with the silent green ahead of you and dark infinity beneath.

I stepped in first and felt the little yacht lean into the river, then regain its balance. I reached up for Jim, where he stood on the jetty, and lifted him in. He was light as bone. I sat him down beside me and the water barely shifted beneath us. Sometimes a heron flapped down and landed on one of the big rocks at the entrance of the river or a bird shrieked out of the bush, but these were the only sounds. We could sit there for hours if we wanted, we were so generously alone. There might be a biscuit we'd eat, that we'd brought with us, or a plum, but mostly we were still. We were dreaming, I suppose. Making plans for leaving. I thought about all the places we could go in the boat, how we could escape the summer-house forever. Our father, badly sunburned with his poor pink eyes, could line up the glasses on the table for cocktail hour and we'd never have to see him. Our mother could be sick again, bringing up those animal sounds, and we wouldn't hear. In our boat we could be safe, quite sure of our destination. It was where we needed to be. As we sat together, the green water before us turning slowly opaque as the clouds deepened, a trout completed – with one leap – a splash, a silver curve. Everything must change.

When the rain came it came first as the scent of rain, the grey air stained darker behind the hills. Then when it came down to us it was like thread and needles, piercing the jellyish water with a trillion tiny pricks, the silver threads attaching water to sky. And there too was the sound of rain, drumming gently upon the canvas cover where it was stretched taut at the back of the boat. It was so warm.

Rain was with us, all around us and in our hair, wetting our skin, trickling down my neck to the centre of my body. Drops of water hit the enamel cup that was there from the days when our father kept all his fishing things in the boat, the bag of knives and hooks, his covered rods. Sometimes my mother used to go out with him.

The two of them rose early when it was still dark, like lovers they left the house and ran across the lawn. The grass might have been damp with dew or dry from night after night of hot moonlight, warm beneath their bare running feet. They must have pushed the boat out, in those days, from the beach, there was no need then to keep it tied up and trapped, they would have pushed it together, fumbling with the ropes in the dawn until the wind caught the sail. Then, in seconds, they were off, swept across the water, night at their backs and the sky paling before them, the light carving out a space around their young faces.

Neither my mother nor my father went fishing anymore. The rain hit the enamel cup with a tiny musical sound, striking the cup, filling it. Drop after drop, the rain. If it rained long enough the cup would be filled with new water. Out across the river rain fell, from behind the hills, rain. Rain into water, rain on leaves. Raindrops dripping from the white blossom of the tea trees, rain sliding down the muddy channels of the riverbank, rain on us. We let it do that, cover us, the sky could weep. My little brother tilted his face up to the last of the light and closed his eyes. Under water he was transparent.

TWO

WE USUALLY CAME to the river when the sky was soft. No other people came there on the misty days and the oily green water curved out of the bush for us alone. At home our parents were playing bridge with their friends in a hot, yellow room. They wouldn't come looking for us. We could stay out all day if we wanted, poking sticks around the roots of trees for eels, sitting on the riverbank wiggling our toes in the water to see if the baby trout would nibble on them.

I had hopes of staying there, I know. It was the sort of thing I'd taken out of books, children going wild, and I imagined that, like them, we could build our own house out of trees with a garden of wild grasses so no one would even know it existed. I thought of all those shiny pictures, the cosy-knit paragraphs of boys and girls who looked after themselves, their fires, their pots boiling with stew. In turn, I saw how we could be as hearty. 'Hey! Over here!'

'I say! What about going off and catching our own fish?'

We'd keep up good cheer no matter if the rains slicked

us down; we might sing. I saw us, smiling there, hands on hips. Nothing could touch us, nothing, no other people. It was almost as if we'd been born unparented. As the months went by we would change, wear quick green outfits woven from softened flax. We would throw away our city things and live instead as true members of the bush. Like trunks, leaves. Our skin tough and brown, and our feet nude.

I look back on those dreams of taking my brother into the bush and of course we had to get out of the house every day, stay away. It was summer, too hot and dirty inside to breathe, and there were so many places at the lake for my brother and I, crescent beaches, inlets. Why be trapped in one garden? If we didn't go upriver, there were patches of silky grass we could lie on, secret among the dried-up paddocks, but we knew where to find them – napkins of green. Or we could cut right back across the farmland and get up onto the hills, climbing the rock face and then following the dusty motorbike trail up and up until we reached the plateau where yellow-eyed sheep kept their distance, groups of them like madwomen in an asylum, watching us half slyly then scattering, messing themselves when we came near. Most days the skies were hard blue and then we spent all day down at the lake, flat on the sand, just the small bees buzzing among the lupins for sound and the soft licking waves remind-ing us of coolness. It was important always to find our own private picnic place, somewhere secret. It may be our own little beach or a part of sand so simple it was just hidden behind a dune – but either way it had to be our own, no other people could be there. That was my obsession, the shyness of bodies, the way my heart rabbited when I heard a transistor, some loud happy voice. I wanted only quietness, the two of us alone together. Queer wishes for a girl.

'Let's go and discover,' said Jim, and that's how it started, our tiny, foolish leaving. 'Please let's go.'

Upstairs, in her room, our mother shifted in her sleep. Quickly my little brother took my hand.

'Don't worry, Jimmy,' I said. 'It's OK.'

It was early morning but it would be hours yet before she would rise. The curtains were drawn, the darkness around her complete. Our father's cups of coffee, set down beside her, only formed skins and went cold and undrunken. She would sleep on.

'From now on we have to look after ourselves,' I told my brother. 'Make a picnic, sandwiches. You tell me what you need . . .'

Outside, the sun was lengthening along the side of the house. Even on the misty days, when the light was pale, you could feel the heat of the day pressing through. By mid-morning the sun might have burned off the cloud and the sky would be clear and blue and polished, not a wisp of white to remind you of the early softness. Then the beach would be crammed with people and there would be boats jetting across the lake, the bladed sound of them cutting down any silence we might have. There would be the noise of families with beach umbrellas and huge coloured picnic rugs, and teenagers running in

15

packs, their giggling together, noisy secrets, their bright, small bikinis. Boys picked girls up whole, waded into the lake, and held them high above the water until they were screaming. They wore racers, like slippery underpants; they were barely covered at all and where they stood you could see the water touching them, leaving a dark stain.

'Hurry up!' I whispered to Jim. Our lunch packet was fixed. It was nearly seven o'clock already and if we wanted to be first, find our private place before those people got there, then we must leave now.

'I *am* hurrying . . .' His voice came from out on the back porch. He was rummaging in the pile of damp bathing things for his face-mask, hidden somewhere at the bottom of yesterday's sandy towels and beachbags and sandshoes. He never did learn how to wear that mask: standing knee-deep in water, peering down on the lake's surface, or swimming with it strapped uncertainly to his head, the eyeglass filling with water every time he took a breath and went under. Still, he loved it, a face-mask was manly, I suppose, and he often used it instead as a little basket, filled with things he'd collected. Shells, bits of flowers and twigs, hooks, and, once, in a jar, a little brown fish with a dead eye that he'd rescued from a drying puddle.

'We can go and discover and have a picnic . . . We can do anything we want.'

To me, he was always five years old – maybe that was part of it. His red shorts were so tiny in those days they could have been made from a handkerchief. I'd put crackers with cheese and apples in a paper bag, and we had a bottle of orange and a chop, too, that had been sitting on the barbeque all night and no one had touched it. There was nothing I couldn't do for him, my own toy, I felt he belonged only to me.

'Do you want a glass of orange, sweetie? A cake?'

I made his supper at night, washed out his clothes, unthreaded the knots from his hair and pulled a jersey over his head when he shivered. I kept chocolate in my pocket for bribes.

'Time to go to sleep now. Finish your lunch first. No you can't.'

'I can't bear it,' my mother once said to me. 'You make me feel so old.'

There was my vanity. Thinking she'd forget about her darling boy if I kept him out of her way, thinking I could keep him. It was me he called out for, but it was her soft hair that brushed across his face when she leaned over him in bed at night.

'Shhh . . .' Light as breath she was kissing him good-night, his own mother. 'Shhh . . .'

Who was I, next to her? Who was I to settle so fully into his belief that I could protect him, when I myself was just another fish-belly kid? Who was I to think my parents couldn't get me if they'd wanted to? All children are powerless against the adults who surround them. We turn from them, set our mouths, but still our soft milk bones yield. They are bejewelled, our parents, they've earrings screwed into their lobes, buckles at their waists. They move amongst each other, the fabrics of their clothing touching, hem to seam, skin joined, lips parting. We have to share their lives, their homes and all their tricks. It's what we're born to. We grow and lengthen, spawn fills our own sacs, and still they want to keep us as their young. We're their living, heaving seed. Proof that they ever loved.

'Darlings!'

Here I am now, remembering. The endless bright days of watery green, sunlight glinting through the thick leaves where we played, the lake behind spread out like pale blue silk. And it's hard to believe so much air and light wasn't enough to keep us fresh. There were long, long days away from the house, rinsed bodies from so much swimming, wet hair sleek on our heads like seals. We had books to read, and comics. Our own food. Why go back at all? Once, long ago, I'd seen my father catch a salmon, hooking it out of a deep fast river, the fish threshing silver with the rushing water all around it. Afterwards, when he'd taken the hook from its lip and slit open the bright guts, he wrapped the body in wet newspaper and cooked it right there on the bank in a fire he'd made. This was way up in the mountains, it wasn't our river, we had to drive to get there. Still, I worked these memories into the story of my brother and me living alone in the bush. Catching old brown trout so slow and fat to move you could practically tickle them out from their holes. Growing sweet potatoes in our wild garden, dye of blackberries on our fingers. Why go back at all? The skin came clean away from the fish and I ate the dense flesh packed beneath. Surely the sweetness of it was enough to live on?

But I was growing up. I think I knew already the whole sad fact of children trying to escape. We're always trying, always thinking: tomorrow. Forever holding our breath in bed, hoping that there'll be an easy death, or hanging out of the windows late at night and wishing that the stars and God and the angels will magic us away.

Wish, *wish* . . . said all the books I read. As if you could make it come true. As if we could be like the shipwrecked boys and girls who prayed for their smoke signals to be seen by a distant ocean liner, or like the wardrobe children who closed their eyes so tight for wishes they saw blood behind their lids . . . As if. Deep down I knew I shouldn't be putting trust in thin stories when all the time we returned, my brother and I, home to our close parents in the end. Besides, it was getting dark. The moon was rising like a lamp and though it was still warm it was late and Jim was hungry. Walking back to the summer-house, along the still edge of beach, we imagined meals like the fancy-coloured pictures in magazines. Plates of fried eggs and vegetables, pies with a frilly crust, trifle. Back at the house there were baked beans he could have, or spaghetti. Anything from a can.

'I imagine some toast,' said Jim Little. 'Perhaps I imagine it. With jam. Perhaps with chocolate spready and jam.'

That was something I could easily do, slip quietly past the adults into the kitchen and make him a sandwich. If we were lucky, no one else would be in there looking for ice or water, asking questions.

'Who feeds you at night, dear? When Mummy's busy?'

'Are sandwiches really enough for a growing boy?'

In the next room the music got louder, some people joined in on the chorus. 'Lo-o-ooove YOU!' they sang.

'What do you children usually have for dinner at night?'

I heard a bottle crash, laughter.

'Something cold, hmmm?' the woman had a voice like a nurse. 'Mummy's leftovers?'

'Darlings!' she cried when, finally, we pushed open the screen door and stepped inside. 'You're home at last and safe!' The room moved with people, all the hot lights turned on. The ashtrays were crowded with the ends of cigarettes, some printed with our mother's bright lip-stick, the pretty colour she wore for parties when she wanted to be very glamorous. There were glasses every-where, full and empty like decorations. Our mother shook her head so her earrings jangled. 'My children . . .' she said, looking around at all her bright friends, smiling for their attention. 'They run around all day like little savages and I never see them at all . . .' She reached for Jim Little but missed him. Her fingertips just brushed his skin. 'Put a shirt on, my baby. Then come and sit on my knee and be a mummy's boy.'

All the world came back at us then. Our quiet and empty day dissolved in the darkness behind us and we were gathered into their noisy crowd, their ashtray breaths in our faces, and our mother so pretty, it was like there was no drink in her at all. Our father's soft red eyes tried to look at us when we came in, but I don't think he really saw.

'Hello-up,' he said. 'What are you two doing at home?'

The record-player was turned on loud for my mother's dancing and how often I saw the silk slip from her tanned shoulders, the six bright bracelets click up and down on her arm as she moved, up and down, up and down, clicking, separating, joining. She was doing the princess dance, the lovely one, looking at some other man, not our father. It was airless in the crowded room, with all the talking, the smoke hanging in the air and swirling in the light of the lamps. . . You could feel a bit sick, to walk in on them, all their painted eyes upon us, but still we were pleased, Jim Little and I were pleased, to see our mother so happy. She was swinging gently to the music as she selected a card, humming along. 'Hmmm, mmm,' she sang. 'I love a man . . .'

Everyone else sat at the table like dummies, their flat cards laid out in front of them. Only our beautiful mother was different, swaying above them, holding her cards in a fan against her, dreamy as a girl.

'You're not concentrating on the game, Kate,' Mr Gordon from next door said, and his hand went out for her.

My mother smiled. Her eyes were lowered so you could see the shine of colour upon the lids, see the long eyelashes, stiffened with black.

'Don't be so silly, Charles . . .' She took a step back, still keeping the cards close against her. 'You know how very well I play.' Still looking at him she fingered them, licking her forefinger and separating the cards one by one. Her hips, sheathed by the silk fabric of her dress, moved slightly. 'No peeking,' she said.

I was still holding my brother's hand, we were two fools just standing there in the middle of the room.

'Can you bear that child?' I heard some woman say. 'I could take him home myself and keep him.'

I felt Jim's grip tighten.

'It's OK, it's OK.'

Then a man with big bulging eyes started coming over towards us. 'Can you kids dance or sing at all?' His shirt was open most of the way down the front and he was waving his glass in time to the music. I saw how pink his stomach was, curling with dark hairs. He leaned towards me and I had to step back so his skin didn't touch me. 'You're a big girl,' he was saying. 'There must be some little party piece you could do.'

There was another crash and someone screamed, 'He pinched me! He pinched me! He really did, the potato!'

I led Jim towards the kitchen. I would make us something to eat, some tidy meal on a tray, which we could take upstairs to our room. If we turned off the lights the adults would think we were sleeping. They wouldn't bother us then, just peek in maybe, two of them together, but when they realized the room wasn't empty they'd leave, trying to tiptoe but making too much noise for that, giggling, bumping into walls.

'Come on,' I said. 'It's late and you're hungry. What would you like for your supper, Mr L?'

We were nearly out the door when in her loveliest voice we heard our mother call, 'Darling, please.' She had left the cards on the table and was flopped down on the sofa, long tanned legs stretched out like she was a model. It was always the loveliest voice when she wanted me to pour for her. Johnnie Walker Red with a rattle, that's what she always wanted from me. I alone knew how to put in six cubes of ice, exactly six, and top up the glass so when you twirled it the ice clinked prettily.

'Listen to him rattle,' my mother said, after her first sip. 'You make Johnnie seem so nice.'

Sometimes she kissed me then, on the mouth, and I left the lipstick stain there as proof that she had done it and because I could imagine, with the fruity taste of it smeared lightly on my lips, that one day I would be a lady too, who would wear earrings that jingled and high gold sandals for parties. I would be my mother's daughter then, made fresh in her mould, fully grown and smooth. I could take a son up on my knee and hold him, feel his wild heart beating in the cage of my arms. My painted nails would trace his mouth, find the pink clean insides of his ears. 'I love you, honey,' I would say.

'Go into the kitchen,' I said to him now. 'I'll be there in a minute. Have a glass of milk.'

'Don't want to . . .'

'Go on, now. I won't be long.'

Instead of leaving, Jim pressed up to me, put his arms around my legs.

'Do what your sister tells you,' someone said. 'Don't be such a naughty boy.'

'Don't want to. Don't want to . . .'

Our mother was still spread out there on the sofa; she'd closed her eyes and there was a tiny smile on her face like she was beginning a dream.

'I don't want to go on my own,' Jim was saying. 'People are in there. I don't want to go to the kitchen at all.'

He was pressed so closely around my legs I couldn't even get to the drinks cupboard, but perhaps it didn't matter now. It really did look like my mother was sleeping. Perhaps she might not notice if I left making the drink for her this one time. Perhaps she might not want it.

'Don't you think you've had enough, Kate?' My father said it often enough. 'Don't you think it's time to wind down for the night?'

I looked over at her again and she seemed quite contented lying there with her tiny smile. Even her breathing was soft and even. 'OK,' I said to Jim. 'Let's go and make your supper. I don't think Mother's thirsty, we can leave the party now and – '

'Wait!' The eyes had snapped open. From where she lay on the sofa our mother was suddenly wide awake, bright and staring as a doll. Slowly she lifted a finger and pointed at me.

'I asked you,' she said, 'to get me a drink.'

For a minute I couldn't move, everything seemed silent and fixed. There was no music, no one else in the room, just my mother looking at me and pointing, and staring with frightening doll's eyes.

'So,' she said, very quietly. 'Get it.'

Suddenly, with a rush, I was all blood. I pushed Jim Little from me so powerfully he fell. 'Get off me!' I left him there to the rest of them, maybe on the floor. Only much later that night when I was nursing him in bed did I imagine how his body could have been trampled, but there was no time for those thoughts then. At the drinks cupboard I found a glass, dirty, rinsed it with water from a jug but my hand was so shaking I spilt it all down my front.

'I'm sorry, I'm sorry . . .'

There was the bottle, the soda, the ice tray with cubes in it. I tried to dislodge them the usual way but I couldn't twist the tray. My mind wasn't going right, the rushing sound was still in my ears, a dark taste at the back of my throat. Finally I banged the tray hard enough on the counter that the cubes fell out. Six. One after the other I counted them into the glass, added whisky to the top of the ice and finished off with soda.

'What a busy girl,' said Mrs McKenzie in a loud voice, putting her arm around my shoulder. 'Helping your mother out with the hostessing . . .' In a whisper, she added 'There now. Chin up. It's not so bad.'

It wasn't until much, much later that Jim and I were finally allowed to leave the party. Someone made Jim sing, a little thing he'd learned at school, but he was so tired by then he was white and his voice came out only in a whisper. I mixed drinks for all the adults who wanted them and the man with the bulging eyes put his hand on my knee.

'Making yourself useful, little lady?'

My mother didn't mean to be that way, I knew that. She loved me. 'Be my valentine?' that's what she'd said, when I'd given her the Johnnie like I should have all along. 'Kiss me?'

She was beautiful, that was all. With her it seemed worse when the worm got in, but really she was no different from anyone else. She was alone too. Scared at how life turns out and with nothing left to do about it. The future wasted and only the past now, rolling up from behind.

Today I understand these things, of course. Years have gone by. Still, there were the seeds of understanding in me then too. I remember, for example, that same night, when my little brother was deep and sleeping, how I got out of bed and went over to the window. It was wide open to the night air. Stars were there, and moonlight shining over the lake so it looked like a fairy thing, a spill of silver, like the moon was tipped clean over and I could see inside it. How much space there was around me that night, though I was at home in my small room, how many pure miles. I stayed so long at the window I saw the moonlight fade and dawn come in. Still I stayed there, empty, hearing only the sound of the water.

'Hush, hush,' she said, though I wasn't crying. 'Hush, hush. Hush, hush.'

THREE

NONE OF THE HOUSES was old. They felt old, when I was a child, blistered paint peeling off, rusted tin roofing patched over in parts with sheets of new red, but really, nothing built on that south-west side of the lake was more than a generation. My father loved to tell that story, of how he chose our property, and how our family came to spend our summers there. Because he alone had access to a few facts, he felt a sense of ownership with them, pride. Stories were his weakness in that way.

What happened was, he said, the land came up for sale all of a piece and some speculator drove up from the city and put a bid in, won it. For a week or so he owned the whole spit, from two miles of river inland all the way down the long beaches on both sides. He could have pointed at the map during that time, to the little finger of white that poked into the blue and thought: mine. What a prize.

That feeling didn't last long, though. In his wide felt hat he wasn't the type to get smoochy about a bit of water and some sand. Before the month was up he'd divided the spit for auction, section by section. He must have been a gold tooth when he retired, people said, a shiner. He knew the value of our summers before we did – the place for tying up boats, the sheltered beaches, fly fishing off the spit at dusk – he saw the money in all of it, glinting like sun.

It was late autumn the day my father made the trip up to the lake for the sale. All along the desert road he had to keep his headlights on, that's how dark the sky was, like steel; any minute he reckoned thunder. There's that quiet big storms bear before they break, and driving along the empty stretch of road he must have felt how small he was beneath the sky, how composed of seconds and minutes, each draw of breath a pulse of blood from the heart. On his left, as he drove, the mountains were like walls. Even though it was still early in the season, there had already been a big snowfall and, though the tops were in cloud, the base of the range was thick with whiteness, gleaming like something from a dream.

Although driving by headlights made it seem like dusk, he arrived at the lake around eleven in the morning, much later than he'd intended. By then it was truly pouring. The storm had broken just as he'd started the long descent Jim and I called 'the bender' – a long corkscrew piece of road that started at the plateau and unwound over three sets of hills that went down to the lake. The last section was the most difficult, just gravel in those early years, and slow and narrow. The chips struck up on the side of the car like bullets and with it raining so hard that the windscreen wipers were swiping back and forth, back and forth, and still not clearing the glass fast enough for him to see more than a couple of yards in front, it must have been slow going for him that morning.

The lake was entirely obscured by water when finally my father pulled up, but still he had the glad lifting feeling of arrival. It was the feeling that visited him always when he got to that carved-out piece of the country – time and place self-contained yet the water seeming to stretch out forever, the feeling from the very first time. He'd always loved the lake, right from when he'd first come to know it as a boy and his own father took him there. They used to stay up on the north end then, in the main town, a good four hours on from the turn-off back in the hills. Though his first sighting of water would have been on the eastern side, different altogether over there with the road close like a band to the water's edge, not so wild, still the feeling for him was the same now as then: I'm here. The ten-year-old's big grin.

Ed, my father's father, was quite famous around the water for his fishing. For someone who was not a local he managed to catch a fantastic amount of fish, trout mainly, rainbows and browns from the lake, but salmon too, in season, the big daddies who coursed the seaward rivers, stung with salt as they swam up towards the fresh. I think he was a poor man. I think he didn't have much time to spend, but still he got to the lake any free days he had and he planned to retire there too. My father said he thought nothing of loading up the old Morris 8 straight after work on a Friday and driving all through the night so he could be at the lake by dawn. That kind of behaviour, back in the thirties, must have earned him a reputation even before he brought the first fish in. Keen wasn't enough of a word for it.

'Tough as well . . .' My father filled up the top of his drink. 'Your grandfather would have scared the living daylights out of you, I know that. Still, you might have got to know him after a while. He could teach you a thing or two.'

We were sitting out in the shade of the back porch. My father had been drinking whisky sours all afternoon and was wanting me to hear all his stories about the old days – how he came to buy the land, and how his father taught him about fish and the lake, and how strong the old man was, how deft with the rod. Beside him, where he sat in the half-broken wicker chair, was a big red plastic bowl full of lemons and a knife. When his drink got low, he leaned over, picked up a lemon and, with the other hand, cut it clean in two, right there in his palm. Then he squeezed the two halves into his glass, added whisky and a lump of ice from the bucket.

'Cheers.'

You can go to the library in town today and look up old newspapers and my grandfather's there, on the inside back page, along with the football results and tennis scores. You can see yellowed pictures of this man from town holding up one of the biggest brown trout ever caught at the lake, a thirty-one-pounder, unbelievable.

ED PHELON DOES IT THIS TIME says the headline, and the column underneath tells the story of the struggle: my grandfather's dinghy just about capsizing as he brings the old fish in, the trace stretching with the weight of him, but safely in the boat by the end, his labour done.

My grandfather used a Dragonfly that famous afternoon, not a favourite fly at all. He felt it was always too heavy, my father said, there was a cheating quality to it that you didn't get with some of the lighter dries – a Wispy, say, or a Doctor McKay's Favourite. Whatever he thought of it, the Dragonfly worked for him that day. He won money and a bottle that was drunk that night, and was known around the lake from then on as a man who, although just a townie, had business to be there.

If you keep going through back numbers of the *Evening News* you find at least two dozen references to my grandfather's luck and skill. Right through the thirties and forties he came up to the lake, fishing not only the northern bays, but also rowing further down to some of the more remote pools on the west where the water was nearly black with reflections from the hills. How quiet it was in those parts, as history, no settlement there at all and never would be. Ed and my father had to clear out a space in the bush with hatchets so they could camp, at night needing their fire, by day fishing the deep pools that lay at the foot of the cliffs.

'The water there was alive,' my father said. 'You could practically feel the trout moving under the boat . . .'

I wondered, when he first told me all this, if he was frightened then? I wonder now, if he prayed, at first, they'd never catch a fish at all, that the line would never jag and hold? I wonder if he was scared of that first wild hiss, when the reel goes crazy, spinning out yards of take so the fish can believe its bid for freedom and can swim far away from the cruel boat, only to stop, feel the hook still in?

'What the hell!'

My grandfather's rod arches and holds, bent so far over that its thin tip touches the skin of the water. It retains for a second longer then the line spins like razors from the reel.

'We're on my boy!'

My father waits, watches. Perhaps he cowers a little at the other end of the boat, silenced by his father's sudden frightening change of mood.

'Come on, you bugger! I've got you now!'

His father sweats, the rod jammed up against him, so strained with the effort of the fish resisting the line you'd think it might snap. He shifts his weight for balance and the boat gives a terrible heave all off to one side, then regains, and he's letting the fish take some line, now winding it back, the rod bending then releasing, the struggle of fins and tail and vertebrae translated into the tension of the man's body, straightened by the rod, reddened, like he's the one suffering pain.

How my own father must have stood by with the net. As the poor thing was brought in, thrashing, drowning in air, my father, as a boy, stood by to take part in the final catching. He had the net steady beneath the fish's long body as it twisted underwater for the last time . . . Then brought it up fast.

'You got him!'

The fish, inches from his eyes, writhed in the string mesh, hooked deep in its pale mouth.

'He's in!'

'What a beauty!'

How many fish did he net for his father in this way? How many rainbows, their lovely gleaming sides of pink and sky-blue leaving new scales on his hands? How many deep browns, those fish mottled and dark as the muddy places where they loved to feed? There were salmon too. Ed took my father up into parts of the river no one else even knew about, showed him where the best sections of the water were – where it took a bend, say, or in the V of a current when two waters joined and formed one channel. There they caught prize quinnat, fat young fish with not a mark on them, slippery pale grey, or others so criss-crossed with scars that you could read on their bellies their age and the river they'd swum against every year to get back to the place where they'd been born.

As the numbers of the *Evening News* advance you start to see pictures of my father appearing. First, there he is, standing next to Ed, a thin kid with a grin, tilting at the camera to show off the fish he's caught. Then there's another picture of the two of them, my father a bit older this time, still with that shaven skinniness to him but taller now, and solemn. You can really see the family likeness in that photo. Same beaky noses, big hands.

Both have the same way of standing, their legs apart and shoulders back. Some old soldier thing of my grandfather's I guess. Stand up like a man. Look the world in the eye. Don't let anyone see you're beat.

For all that, he never did get to retire to the lake like he'd planned. He was coming home from work one night, just the same as any other night, and dropped dead of a heart attack right there in the driveway.

'That's the way to go,' my father said. He squeezed another half-lemon into his drink. 'Bang. Finish. No more surprises.'

By now it was late in the afternoon. The sun was so high behind the house it couldn't stay true. Already it had ripened and the blue sky around it was turning gold in the last big heat. Beyond the shade of the porch everything burned. The grass, the lemon rinds tossed along the fence line. I so wanted to be back at the beach with my brother. The water was warm this time of day, in the shallows bright turquoise and all the little fish like sequins. We could float like starfish among them, then swim up to our favourite place by the bay, and the sand there would be rich and thick to lie on.

I hadn't even expected to find my father on the porch. Usually, on sunny afternoons, he slept inside or lay on the lawn with my mother if she was sunbathing. All I'd done was come back to the house for suncream. I never wanted to stay, and as I was running through the front door I heard him call out. 'Janey, that you?'

I stopped. Through the open kitchen window I could

see him sitting there, the back of his head and those dry folds of skin around his neck. The bowl of lemons set down beside for company. 'You know something,' he was saying. 'Right here, where I am, you could say it's a piece of your family history . . .'

There was nothing else I could do. I crossed the room and went out onto the shadow of the porch.

'What do you mean?' I said.

'I'm telling you . . .' He took a sip from his drink. 'This house, our connection to the lake . . . It's all to do with your grandfather, my father. And of course it's to do with your mother too . . .'

That was when I knew I'd have to stay. He would talk on and on about his father and his boat, how many fish were caught, how many miles were travelled over water, but always the story couldn't finish without the same ending.

You see, he had to get to that sale. He'd driven through the storm, through the black air with his headlights turned on, needing all his time. Back in the city he'd just asked my mother to marry him. She was a girl who wore her clean hair brushed back, and there was about her then the cool smell of lavender. My young father couldn't stop thinking about her. She didn't know the lake then, she'd never been there at all and now my father could offer it to her as a prize. So, like his father before him, he drove for hours at a fever. The money was in his pocket. It was some fairytale, wanting to buy a piece of land as a wedding present for his bride.

He arrived at the lake that morning in the pouring

rain. A group of men in heavy sou'westers were standing around under a makeshift canvas awning that had been strung up between two cars. The sale had begun at nine and already sixteen of the twenty sections had been sold. My father opened the car door and, with no coat and his head down against the weather, he ran across the muddy paddock to where the men were gathered.

'Left it a bit late, haven't you?'

He was wearing his good suit and in the few seconds it had taken to cross over to them the rain had soaked it through. It clung to him like cotton.

'Jim Phelon,' he said, there was water running down his face. He put out his hand to shake hands with the man sitting behind a trestle table covered with maps, with plans of the land and how it had been divided. 'I telephoned you a couple of days ago about Section 14. You gave me a figure and I've the money for you now if you've had no other takers.'

The rain drummed on the canvas roof, sluiced down the sides. Men in wet coats jostled against each other for room.

'Thing is, Mr Phelon, I've taken a bid on that property already. Chap right beside you, in fact. Just five minutes ago.'

All the other men were prepared for the sale, they'd dressed for the weather. Only my father, not able to get off work the day before, had had to drive through the night to get there for the early start. The others had arrived in easy time, walking up and down the whole length of the spit to gauge it, checking boundary lines against the map, listening to what the man at the table had told them about septic tanks and water bores. They looked at him now, a young man in thin clothes, his wet, muddy shoes. No one said a word.

'What happened then?' I said.

My father leaned back in the chair. 'Well . . .' His face was tired from the drinks and the heat. 'I was worried, I'll tell you that much. It was Number 14, you see. It had to be Number 14. I'd seen the plans in the paper when I'd read about the sale and I knew that was the property for me. There were only two good sections left, out of the whole lot of them. This one, and another one up by the river, only I knew it would be too dark there for your mother, I wanted her to have the sun. Number 14 was wide open to the water and no other houses could be built there. She could go right up to the window and see clean across the lake. Nothing could take that view away . . .'

He shifted in his chair, tipped his glass slightly like he was checking for a whisky level but thinking about something else. 'It was all the money I had in the world, right there in my pocket. That was the property I needed to buy.'

I looked up at him, where he sat. The skin around his eyes was creased from squinting. I knew the end of the story, still, I asked again, 'What then, Daddy?' He expected it. 'What then?'

My father took a big pull of his drink. 'I told the guy the truth.' His voice was thick and syrupy now, most of the bottle was gone. 'I told him just like I've told you. I said, "I'm getting married", I told him the whole story.'

He drained off his glass. 'There I was, soaking wet, I didn't even have a coat and rain was pouring down my suit, it was probably my only suit, and I tell you what, I pleaded with the guy. I begged him. He knew the value of the land, he was no fool. Still, he did me a favour that day. He cancelled his bid, drove back up north. And so you're sitting here right now not him.' My father reached down to cut another lemon. '1960 we built this place, the year you were born. That's what I mean . . . Family history . . .'

I was ready to go then. It was something about the light, the way it had changed. Something about the smell of the drinks, old, turned by the sun, the pile of wrung out yellow rinds gathered at my father's feet. I'd already been with him too long. Still, he talked on, his voice getting drowsier and drowsier, like he was talking to himself. 'We put the foundations in the year your mother was expecting you . . . The land's protected . . . Prime real estate . . . A house for all our summers . . .' He cradled his empty glass, his eyes were closing. The rotted chair, used to him, took his weight as he sank deeper and deeper. 'Number 14 . . . Had to be . . . She was so happy then, when she saw it . . .'

He was asleep. Quietly I edged past him, stepping over his glass, the bowl. Things were all about him, old things, new. Chairs, empty bottles, an oar from a boat, torn nets . . . all piled up in the back porch because there was nowhere else for them to go. I found the bottle of suncream I'd come for in a plastic bag in the pile of towels and T-shirts beside the door. So many things. It was our life; those boxes of gumboots, mouldy raincoats on hooks. As I ran off back to the beach I realized that from where he sat, after all his story, my father couldn't even see the lake. He was sitting on the wrong side of the house. There was no view there.

FOUR

'LET ME STAY UP and play, let me. I want to get into your bed, I had a bad dream.'

My little brother is suddenly standing beside me, his face moon-white in the darkness.

'We could go outside and play,' he is saying. 'It's cleaner there. We could go swimming or do any kind of playing. Oh, Janey, please? Please let's go. I hate it here.'

It's late, past midnight, and I've twisted my one sheet. I don't think I was asleep, I think I was just lying here. The heaviness of the air feels like drugs and my voice when I speak has a crust on it.

'Jimmy, you should be sleeping . . .' I start to sit up in bed then stop. 'It's not good for you to be walking around the house at this hour. There are too many people here. You know it's safer in your own room, darling.'

He clasps his hands together, 'Please . . .' His body trembles slightly and the cowboys and indians on his short pyjamas gallop all over him. 'I'm not sleepy at all,' he whispers. 'Please do let's go outside.'

He often comes in to me like this late at night, I can't stop it; I could run myself. Out there it's open and cooler than this hot room enclosed. We could go for a swim, we could play. There's no need to cling here when we have so many hours until dawn.

'But it's late,' I say. 'And you could be having a nice dream – not a meanie. You could be sleeping like an elf on a leaf, breathing slowly in and out, remember? The way I taught you?' He nods, believing, and I feel myself the liar. You'd think I was his mother the way I talk to him. She might calm him this way with pretend, she'd have the gift to make him sleep.

'Sleep, sleep, my little Jim Little . . .'

His eyes would close.

'Sleep, sleep, my baby boy . . .'

The truth is, how can either of us be restful when downstairs the noise of people at my parents' party is like water in a dungeon? Their voices smack and rumble, they laugh and the sound of it slops up and hits against the walls. We should be used to the parties by now, my brother and I, but we can still hear monsters in them.

'Oh stop it, I'll die!'

And a man replying something guttural.

'Don't do that!'

The smell and smoke of all the people rises up in a yellow wave, up the stairs, along the hallway to where Jim Little and I keep our rooms. There's a cheer from below, someone winning with the cards.

'I didn't cheat,' a woman shrieks. 'I'm no bloody liar!'

It may seem quieter where we are now, in my dark blue room, but we're not so far away. People come upstairs all the time, they've forgotten where they are, or they're looking for the bathroom. They could so easily come into our room, flick on the light.

'Surprise!'

They would love too much a boy in Wild West pyjamas.

He quivers in them now, little twig, but not with cold. The thin fabric of the short sleeves curves away from his arms.

'I can't breathe because my mind is hot and bothered,' he says. 'Can't we please go out the window like we always do?'

I look up to where the curtain shifts against the wall, the sky with stars beyond it. A bloom of breeze ruffles the white sheets on my bed and I can feel the heat in it, the sun hidden maybe, but only hours away. The warmth of the day is still contained in the packed, dried earth outside, a baked jar I could put my cheek against. I imagine how its texture might feel like a man.

It's not always this way. Often my brother and I do sleep, right through the late, dangerous hours. The noise and music will surge and swell below us, but we float on it some nights, we don't hear those people drinking. Adults will tell you too that fact about water and sunshine, how together they work upon children a particular exhaustion. After a while of lying there on your bed you can make yourself believe it's true. You feel how swimming really has used away your muscle so your limbs are wasted, your bones softened and dissolved.

You're left just drifting like rags on dark water. Those nights may be best of all.

Not awake to the things that may happen we're protected. Unseeing, unhearing, we're safe against the people who come creeping, who huddle like witches there at the doorway of Jim Little's room.

'See how sweet he is,' they whisper.

'I'd like to wake him up and kiss him.'

'Do you want to?' My mother detaches herself from them. 'Shall I get him up and we can bring him down?' She walks towards him where he lies. 'He's lovely when you pluck him straight from bed. So warm . . . And his skin smells like cake.'

She might laugh then, a spilt laugh across the rest of them, like a river. I don't know why, but everything feels better then, like daylight, when she's happy and I don't believe she would let any harm come to a child. Her pretty laugh flows over the other voices and winds about them, making islands of their talk, my river. Her laugh breaks across the sand, the crinkled water glinting and winking in the sunshine. She's smiling for her children, not for anybody else. We're the ones who love her.

'Come on over here,' she says to us. 'Now, open your mouth and close your eyes . . .'

I tilt my head back so my mouth is like a cup; I feel something small laid in it, a chocolate maybe, or a cocktail biscuit dipped in spread.

'. . . And in your mouth you'll find a surprise!'

Jim Little blinks as he chews and swallows, quickly,

like it's a pill. I eat slowly because I'm older, I smile at my mother when I'm done, at her bright face.

'Thank you.'

There was something sickish in the chocolate, it broke in my mouth. Brandy or wine, a thick adult taste in the sweetness.

'Can we go now?' says Jim. 'I don't want any more of that food.'

Instead of replying, my mother just strokes his neck, her middle finger kneading at the hollow of his nape. Already her thoughts are drifting; she's thinking of something else. She turns to the woman beside her, to silly Mrs Edmonton with watery eyes, and starts talking to her, but in a low voice. Mrs Edmonton nods and smiles a secret smile.

'Between you and me, Betsy,' my mother is saying. 'I'm mad about the boy.'

This all happening before, maybe tonight, maybe another night, I can't remember. There are parties every night. How can I remember the ones my brother and I are called into like little dogs? Maybe it was tonight, I don't know. Other nights we're not needed at all. We have our sandwiches upstairs and glasses of orange, and I get Mr Little ready for bed. If we can't sleep then, we just go out the window. That's often our routine. There's a trellis to climb down on to and we don't even disturb the small half-dead things that grow there. No flowers, no soft fruit to spoil . . . We slide down the smooth wooden frame and land on the grass like pods. Nights like these the darkness is so wide, so open to the moon, I feel I could run off bare to the lake like I used to, no one would see, and I'd love to have my body back like that, to feel it in the air a ribbon. But I'm nearly teenaged now and I must wear jeans, I change into them from my pyjamas. Only my little brother can run clean along the road, bare feet, cotton pyjamas unbuttoned to the night air.

'I'll race you to the water!'

How I want to catch him, be his stop. He flies towards me and I scoop him up, hold him, twine him in to me like wire.

'Ride on my shoulders, Jimmy,' I say. 'Climb on up and I'll be your camel, you can ride me to the beach and build pyramids from the sand.'

I pick him up, put him down. I make him walk on my feet, hold hands, sit him on my back, anything to be close like one body. When we get down to the lake I swing him by his arms in a circle over the waves.

'Aeroplane man!'

'Don't drop me, Janey!'

'Dive!'

'I'll drown if you do.'

The sand where we play on those empty nights is warm, the water tepid. We glide into the shallows like eels, the silky black water parting, closing behind us without a sound. On into the deep we swim, out to where the lake is lapping into endless night, slipping away from us, always further and further, until even the dark sky is filled with stars and water.

Lying on the beach after our swim, my dumb jeans are

sodden. Jim sifts sand against his bare skin, his pyjamas strewn around the beach like petals, while I lie beside him, beached, an old log. In films and TV girls swim in jeans, their boyfriends coming behind, but once the water has covered them to the neck, they slyly undress, zip and bra strap and panties, they feel each other's smooth bodies touching. Their limbs waver towards each other like weeds; his arm hooks lightly around her hips, their legs wind snaky together. There's the soft sound too of sucking when they kiss. It seems not fair they can be so light in water, not fair they're not bound in cloth and towel. Clothes can destroy a swimmer, I know, but I'm not like those puberty girls, I don't want any of those other things happening to me. I've planned it, I'll never know a boy. It will always be only my brother I'll care for, he needs all my attention and I have no time for the other part. Kids at the lake can behave that way if they want: the girls I've seen doing their slow walk up and down the beach, they can cast themselves about, eyes lazy in the sunshine. Those girls in bikinis, arranging themselves on towels for tanning, I don't have to know them. They can smooth on oils. I promise, hope to die, Jim Little, I'll never be like that. I've removed myself from the thought of it. I want to play with you. I want to run out of the smoky house and into the air with you.

Tonight, though, I can't do it. The weight of my own body holds me down, I can't be a floating, curving girl. I'd have to keep my eyes on that little stick splashing about at the edge of the dark water, pull him back when he goes out too deep . . . Tonight, I won't let him go into the water, I won't let him go outside at all. It would be criminal to want to take off my wet clothes while he innocently plays, wicked to want to lie secretly with myself while a child out there in the lake could be drowning.

'Not tonight, Jimmy,' I say. 'You've already been asleep, remember. If you went outside to play now you'd only wake up your poor heart. Let your body rest, sweetie, it's tired all over. Come on now . . .' I peel back the sheet so he can get in beside me. 'You know you can sleep with me if you're frightened . . .'

He scrabbles in next to me and lies curled in my side, breathing lightly at first then more slowly, evenly. It won't be long now until he's asleep. I start telling him a story off the sleeve of his pyjamas about a cowboy meeting a little indian boy and they decide to be friends. Back in the desert their parents are killing each other with muskets and bows and arrows, but the two boys find a plan to make peace. I've just got to the part where the indian goes to see the wise man in his tribe when I see my little brother's head heavy on the pillow. I kiss him once on his dry lips, then pick him up, a tiny bundle of sleep, and carry him back to his own bed. He won't wake again. I know his sleeping so well.

When my mother first brought him home from hospital, the smallest baby, his eyes were sealed waxy. He seemed completely self-contained, closed in his own world. At first, she couldn't leave him alone. She was always unbuttoning her blouse for his feeding, always wanting to open up his muslin wrappings so she could look at his tiny poached parts. Still, he slept on, even while she picked him up from his crib and passed him around so that strangers could hold him.

'I never thought I'd do it again,' she used to say, 'have another baby. But now I feel so clever. I feel I've won him in a cracker as a prize.'

It lasted quite a while, I think, that full feeling she had for him in the beginning. Tiptoeing into the baby's bedroom to watch him sleeping, not believing she'd allowed this little thing to live. She sang to him, she gave him her fifth finger to suck when she had no more milk. She jiggled him on her knee until his eyes startled open like marbles. I was seven years old then and from my distance watched the whole play. Already I myself had a part, already connected to this baby's small life. I watched him as he turned on his blanket in the sun, his pale cheeks to the light, fists tight as rosebuds.

'Do you know who I am?' I whispered to him. 'Do you know my name?'

When my parents started to go out again at night I felt more acutely the weight of my attention. By the time the door shut behind them the first time, I'd already seen my mother with him enough to know what I should do, but still, alone with him, he felt so delicate and precious it was like the air itself might damage him. I fed him from a bottle and bandaged him with nappies and pins. I picked him up all to myself, my face so close I could smell his sweet, milky breath. He was Jim Little from the beginning and I felt such ownership for him that I was the one now who stood by in the darkness and watched him sleep. It seemed I could never tire of the responsibility for that shallow, even breathing.

I stroke his hair now, feathery against the pillow. His lips, nose, brow . . . Each feature is perfectly moulded, cool in the moonlight, cast over with a slight flush from dreaming. How grown he is, already five years old. How long now before sickly adolescence claims him, claims us both? Thickens the blood, turns a quick run into those girls' slow roll?

Back in my own bed, I draw up the sheet. The night is too lonely – no shadows making stories on the wall, no more games to play. My door is half open and the yellow light of the hall falls in a rectangle on my bedroom floor. Through the rising tide of voices downstairs I can make out individual hands and heads sticking up out of the waves, waving, calling, 'I'm over here!'

Night after night, the same people mesh and join in the wash; this is their version of time. They talk and dance, move in and out amongst each other, believing, with every fresh move, that there's something in the evening that will change them.

Women put on make-up, dab themselves with scent in secret places. Men stand by like young animals and the hot record turns, burns in its groove.

C'mon, baby . . . You know I love you . . .

I think what cramped dances they must make together, those husbands and wives, so much hope gone into the night. For all of them there's a moment when glamour begins, holds them ageless in a whirl of lights and lipstick smiles and music. It's the moment when they seem so perfect, but so small.

Are these minutes or hours passing? What night is this, how long have I been lying here?

There are footsteps coming up the stairs. I can hear them coming closer, quiet footsteps. Up to the landing and pausing, up again, closer, they're in the hall. This one is a familiar. He knows exactly what he's come for. Now he moves silently down the hall, stops, stands silhouetted in the door, one man. My wild heart starts up beneath the sheet, I think I know who he is. In the darkness he's a shadow, taller than he should be. Perhaps, I hope, he might be someone else. I must be quiet now, must not move. Not a breath, not a sound. There's the image of a baby sleeping while wolves howl around it, red tongues lolling . . . I want that to be me. Let me be a pebble, a pillow . . . Some still object, not a girl. I feel the blood will burst in my veins I'm so quiet and unmoving, he can't believe I'm awake, but still the man whispers, 'Janey? You there? Sweetheart, it's me . . .'

I know him, my wild heart is beating. It's Bill Cady, Mr Cady, he's from the house down on the point.

'Janey? Honey?'

He's new at the lake this year, looking for a friend, my mother said. I should sit up in bed and politely say hello.

'It's me . . .'

He bought the Donalds' old place way up at the end of the spit, the part where the sand disappears in a finger and it's nothing but water. One man in that big house, no wonder he comes drinking around my parents' every night.

This is my daughter, Bill.

Cady, have you met my children?

Darling, ask Billy if he wants another drink.

'You asleep?' he whispers now. 'Or just pretending, honey?'

The outline of him is narrow and thiefish in the dark. I thought he was supposed to be an old man, much older than thirty, but I know from the way he holds his body he doesn't believe that to be true. He stands poised there in the yellow light of the hall. In the brightness he won't be able to see my eyes, glittering wide awake in the darkness. Perhaps he'll think I'm asleep and I can pretend, when I have to meet him again, that none of this happened at all.

'Oh, come on now. Don't be a spoilsport . . .' He starts walking towards my bed but stops, retreats. Someone's coming.

There's another set of footsteps in the hall. I can hear them, click-click, light steps, I know without seeing her it's my mother.

He turns, 'Why, Kate . . .'

In a second she's beside him at the door, silent as a knife.

'Shhhh . . .' She puts one finger to her lips, every detail of her finely outlined against the yellow of the hall. Her nose, forehead, lips are cut in a delicate edge, turned towards him.

'Kate, I – ' He starts but she stills it.

'Shhhh. Be careful,' she whispers. 'I don't want her to wake . . .'

Quietly, like a fold, my bedroom door is closed, sealed by a tiny clip as the sneck finds its hole. I wait, I breathe, then I hear their footsteps retreating down the hall. They've gone. All I hear is a man and a woman walking away, down the stairs. As they reach the bottom I hear my mother cry out, 'Look who I've found!'

The darkness, now I'm closed in, is complete. Slowly my eyes become accustomed to it – the chest of drawers, the wardrobe, the frame of the mirror against the wall. Poor idiot girl, what am I thinking? People will get drunk at any party, come stumbling in, my mother, a hostess, will come after. What am I thinking that Mr Cady would rouse himself to come to me, wake me? Do I think I'm one of those girls, with their slow roll? Do I think I'm so full and lovely? I imagine things, that's all. I dream. That's why my heart jumps, and blood rushes in my head – because I'm so stupid; I have bad dreams.

'Go to sleep, now . . .'

There's my mother again, with me, we're alone. Her breath is warm over my face but her voice sounds far away.

'Go to sleep . . . Go to sleep.'

She strokes my head, with her fingertips closes my eyes.

'I love you, mother.'

'Shhh . . .' she whispers. 'You're in darkness now. You're my dreaming girl. I don't want you to wake.'

I WAS SENT ON swimming lessons when I was young. I was very soft then. My father believed, maybe he still does believe, that learning to swim can save a life, that it can protect you. He was always telling my brother and me about fishing accidents, children swept out to sea on a freak tide, their mouths opening and closing for air but there being none. He didn't know how many drownings there had been at the lake; too many boats had gone down, he said. They set out in the morning, innocent, but the pale sky turned on them. Storm winds, bad tides. It could be the middle of summer but there was the drop of temperature, a dark shivering in the waves, and suddenly you saw you were far away from land. Treacherous. That was the word my father used about the lake. In it I could hear all the stranded ice of winter water.

I was about four or five when I was sent to the Swimming Institute. Old enough to speak but not so old, Daddy said, that I had lost my gills. The water would open them up for me again, he soothed me, the night before my first time. I thought I was going to die.

'Come on now and no nonsense. Don't you think I've seen lots of little girls' bodies before?'

I nodded, I whispered agreement. I remember every detail of that first day, how I lifted my arms over my head and let the nurse remove my dress, pull down my white pants that were left plopped shamefully on the wet concrete of the changing rooms, someone else's secret.

'That doesn't matter one bit,' she said, she was holding the crotch of my new swimsuit open so I could step into the legs. 'Lots of little girls have accidents here, it usually happens on the first day but no matter. You'll be in the water in a jiffy and nicely cleaned off. Just tell me next time when you want to go to the toilet, hmm? I'll take you to the special little place.'

I held her hand so tightly as she led me to the swimming pool, there was no choice but to trust. My mother was far away, sitting high up in the gallery with the other mothers looking down at the shining, shifting square of blue. I wondered, could she even see me? There were so many children already in the water, splashing, shouting, how would she know that I was not one of those? The tiled edge of the pool was slippery under my bare feet and the smell that came up from it, like disinfectant, made me think of school and how it was to be part of a crowd. At that moment I knew my mother couldn't save me. She'd think I was happy there, playing. She'd think I belonged to another.

'Take a breath! One – two . . .'

As I walked with the nurse the safe end of the pool

was left further and further behind us, the handrails for babies, the thin waters that wrapped softly around your knees. Instead she was leading me to where it was deep, that adult part, where the measurements were marked out in black paint along the side. 6ft. 8ft. 12ft. I knew what the numbers meant, the slick surface of the water told it: Out of your depth. Over your head. The blue so smooth it would be a ceiling.

'Arms over! Stretch!'

There was a man standing right at the end of the pool by the high diving-board. He was shouting out, he seemed angry with someone. We were walking towards him.

'Take a breath! Three – four ... Long gliding strokes ...'

His voice was like armies. It echoed off the concrete walls and came back in hundreds.

'Take a breath! Hold it! Count, one – two. Three – four ...'

The nurse's big hand was pink and plump as a ham. I dared not ask her for my mother now, where she was, whether she was even sitting up there somewhere or whether, in her lovely coat and boots, she had crept away.

'Take a breath!'

As we got closer to him I saw he didn't wear a shirt at all. Across his stomach ran a deep line and the skin was puckered around it, pulled in like a seam. Beside me the water plunged, no shelf, no ledge, no place for me to stand . . . Still, the man's mark at that minute took up my fear. It had turned his whole belly purple.

'New recruit!' The nurse released my grip and pushed me forward to meet him. 'Jane Phelon.'

The man smiled, 'A littley, eh?'

He looked at me from where he stood, his head on one side. Then suddenly he reached forward, took my arm in his fingers. He squatted down beside me and whispered. 'Tasted water before?'

I could feel his breath in my ear.

'Because, Missy, you will have had a few glassfuls of it before this afternoon is over.'

I found out later that the mark on him was an old war wound, the other children told me, or a bite from a shark. When Mr Petersen got angry, they said, it throbbed. He clutched it then as he shouted out our names.

'Lane number two! Number seven! Get out of the water! Get over here and I'll show you what swimming is!'

He flicked the bad ones over the head, took their thin arms and, like pleaching, twisted them into the shape of swimming. He held in one hand a whole head and turned it down and to the side, down and to the side, like a ball on a pivot, to show how a person should be breathing.

'Like this!' he shouted as he did it. 'And like this! How do we do it?'

'Take a breath,' someone said, one of the boys.

'One – two,' whispered another.

'Release it, count, three – four.'

It took me a few afternoons to learn exactly what those words meant, how they were a chant to help you take in air and expel it, how they helped you remember your strokes, showed you what to do. The other part of the lesson was quick. I learned it at the beginning.

'I have one thing to tell you right now,' Mr Petersen said to me that first afternoon. 'The human body floats. Get it? You're like a ball, no matter how deep you go you're going to pop back up on to the top of the water again. Now I want you to take a deep breath . . .'

I inhaled from the bottom of my stomach like my father had taught me – and he pushed me in.

That was the theory at the Swimming Institute: No half measures. Overcome weakness. Learn courage. They were phrases that had come out of some book and men believed in them. Fear was an engine, that was another. The idea was you could start it up and make it roar.

'Institute boys and girls are achievers in so many ways . . .' my father said. 'Not only in the water.'

He was in his study, the letter saying I had been accepted for swimming lessons was in front of him on the desk. He was engrossed in it, reading it over and over, so pleased I was going to the place where he himself had learned.

'Start off in the water and test yourself, that's the thing,' he said. 'Face up to your doubts.'

He unscrewed his pen, humming to himself.

'Strong swimming is a skill you keep with you for life.'

'But I don't want to go!' I think I was crying. 'I want you to teach me!'

He didn't look down.

'Don't be silly, you'll love it. Just you wait and see . . .'

I watched him sign the cheque, put it in an envelope, bang the flap with his fist to seal it.

'Anyway,' he said. 'It's too late. The thing is done.'

I was ill afterwards. For days I kept vomiting water and I could feel the chlorine laying at the bottom of my belly when I ate. In dreams I remembered it, the air going out of me with the force of the push, even before I hit the surface of the pool, and the break of the water itself, the second between air and water, so sharp . . . There was pain in me when I went down. I remembered blackness too, of clenched eyes first, that first black fright, then the simple black endlessness of falling. Nothing else. Beneath the flat, impassive surface of the pool . . . There was my nightmare.

'Get her out!'

The next thing I remember was a wrench, something pulling. As my body rose to the surface I felt an arm, one of the elder children had caught me, pulled me to the side. Air touched my face, I opened my eyes. There was the long strip of lights high on the ceiling.

'That's the worst part over, Missy,' Mr Petersen grinned at me as he lifted me clean out of the pool. 'Now I want you down at the shallow end and jumping in. Just you watch. You won't be able to make your body sink again if you try.'

That was it then, finished. An act fashioned to contain truth, over in minutes – a father loves that kind of lesson. Of course, after losing myself in the deep end, Mr Petersen was right.

The shallows were like a bath. I went down to join the line of children who, one by one, jumped over the side, disappeared for a second in a splash, then rose to the surface again. There was nothing to the game. Even I couldn't wait to take turns, scrambling up the side of the pool, hurrying to be next. In me I held a feeling, like something in a lovely box. Safety? Knowledge? Something light sitting next to the place where I breathed. I loved the way it made white bubbles form a wreath around me underwater, pale chlorine stain my eyes.

'Look at me!'

Some of the boys shouted too as they jumped.

'Dive-bomb!'

'Charge!'

'Going – going – gone!'

When we'd worked on the exercise, over and over again, Mr Petersen came to us and told us what the chanting meant. We stood on the tiles by the shallow end of the pool and he demonstrated, his body bent at the waist, arms outstretched in front of him and his head down.

'Take a breath and hold it. Count, one – two.' As he spoke he slowly pushed back imaginary water with one arm, brought it up so it curved above his head.

'Stretch . . .' He bent his arm then straightened it, from a branch it became an oar. He slid it parallel to his other arm until the fingertips of his two hands met, touched, then the second arm repeated the motion in turn, pushing down slowly through the air. 'Release your breath, now count, three – four,' he said. 'Release it . . .' Up came his second arm and over, forming again the lovely curve, a perfect reflection of its brother. 'Then long, gliding strokes . . .'

Smoothly, evenly, he began again the lovely sequence of slow motion. I didn't yet understand what it meant for swimming but already it seemed a poem to me, the elegance of him, the gorgeous craft of the man in air.

'We'll make a swimmer of her, Mrs Phelon,' Mr Petersen smiled at my mother. 'She's puny now but we'll have her doing lengths with the big boys in no time. Tell your husband.'

It was the end of the first lesson and the nurse had dressed me again, my mother had come for me like she'd never been away.

'Oh, I will tell him,' she said, and she put her hand out for him to take it. 'Thank you very much, Mr Petersen. We'll see you next Tuesday . . .'

One hour twice a week, fifteen minutes on either side to change, for five years my father wanted me to go. All those beliefs, taught by rote, how to breathe, how to push, how to propel yourself at speed through the water while the boat behind you burns . . . They're lodged into me, they live with me. Me. And now I never go near the water. As the lessons went on I learned how to form the smooth strokes of the others, to lie my ear flat on the water and make the neat intake of breath. I learned to turn my ankles inward and kick like the paddles of a duck's foot, to breathe in water like I breathed in air. I pressed my throat and imagined I could feel openings there, fine, fine slits. It was just as my father wanted.

'That's great, honey.' He'd asked me to pull up a chair and show him how I could swim. Lying flat on my stomach on the seat my arms were free to make circles in the air, my legs kicking behind. 'This summer you can lifeguard your mother and me . . .'

The gaps between the afternoons in the concrete chamber, shadows on the walls reflecting the surface of the pool, and light, hot days at the lake . . . The gaps are huge. By the time Jim Little was old enough for swimming lessons I no longer went and my parents' lives had changed too much for them to want to continue with old habits.

'All those things you've been taught,' my mother said. 'You can easily show them to your brother.'

My father nodded. There was no talk about survival by then, just living. Jimmy and I hardly saw either of them during the long days. They stayed around the summer-house mostly, sleeping, maybe scratching a little at each other, I don't know; they were private. With no one to watch over me at first I didn't venture out too far into the lake; after the circumference of the pool in town it seemed too lush and wide. Instead I practised by swimming along the edge of the shore, keeping out at a distance of fifteen, maybe twenty feet. There the water was clear and alive to my open eyes. Sometimes I saw fish in it, their bright rainbow sides, but mostly just the yellow light finding gaps in the water so it lit up in places like glass. I could swim to the river this way, straight up the line of the first beach, past the stand of dead trees that clustered like crucifixes. Or I could turn and go down the right side of the spit where rocks jutted out of the bush and the beach was just a thin frill right at the edge. Either direction, the tides were always changing. The face of water showed no expression of the motions beneath it and often while swimming I surprised myself by grazing sand. I stood up then, and though I might be far away from the beach the water only came up to my thighs. I was ten or eleven at this time. Hands on my hips, I surveyed the miles of water around me and felt so powerful I could have been a boy.

My brother was small during those early years. Courage flowed through me instead.

'Lay your ear on the water,' I instructed him. 'And kick your feet, just your feet not your legs. Take a deep breath, hold it . . .'

He was like a skinny little fish, slippery in my arms. As my parents had told me, I tried to show him the things I had been taught, my secrets, knowledge stored, but he was always wanting to be off on his own, diving in and out of the small waves; he loved doing that.

'Watch me! Watch me!'

He stood there for a second, in my memory I can see him, his hands together like he was praying, the lake holding him sweetly at his waist.

'OK?'

He took another big breath and went under. There was a shower of water, the twin flowers of his bare feet amongst it, then he was standing again.

'You seen me?'

When he was old enough for me to leave him playing there I used to take myself out to where it was deep. I would swim right out past the shelf and over the edge to where the lake changed colour, opening out into such loneliness of depth that it turned the water a dark, heavy blue. In it I could see nothing at all and I would have stayed there for a long time were it not for the cold, arctic, rising from somewhere deep and frozen in the earth. As I swam back towards the beach I often saw Jim jumping up and down, waving his arms. He was scared. I had been out too far.

'You're supposed to look after me,' he said. As I walked through the shallows back to the beach he ran straight past me into the lake. 'I want you to watch *me* swim.'

At the Swimming Institute, I remember, Mr Petersen had a pole with a hook. The weak ones he kept by the side of the pool and when they started to fail in the water he would hook them up by the back of their swimsuits, the hook in a shoulder-strap or under the rim of elastic around the legs, and fish them up on to the side.

'How you breathe,' he said, taking a head in the familiar way, twisting it from side to side. 'It's like this. And like this . . .' Sometimes then he would call us all out of the water, have us stand, shivering, in a line while he told us some story about the war, or when he was young, but there was always a moral to the story. There was always water in it. Sometimes too he would stomp around and yell, about how all of us were plug stupid, that we couldn't get by in open water for ten minutes if he wasn't there, that without him we'd be lost.

'What are you?' he'd yell then, anguish in his voice like his wound was pressing in.

'We're all failures,' we'd have to say.

'What's that? Louder!'

'We're all failures, Mr Petersen.'

This is the part I'm left with, to understand. I had these things in me, the hook, my father with his money out twice a week.

'Go!' Mr Petersen shouted.

There was the sick stone of exhaustion in my stomach as I stood on the diving platform, white toes curled over the edge of it, whole body in a rictus of cold.

'Lane eleven. Go!'

I learned stamina, endurance . . . By the time I was ten I could swim easy lengths by the hour. I became from Lane eleven, Lane four, then two. And here I am now, all method in me. My parents' dry survivor.

'Teach me, Janey? Teach me?'

You'd think I could have managed any tide, any treachery. You'd think I could have shown my brother how.

'He's a natural in the water,' my father used to say. 'And anyway, Janey, it's what I paid your lessons for. You can teach him the rest.'

So I knelt by his still body on the sand. I took his head and I rolled it gently to the side and back, back and around, a ball on a pivot.

'Take a breath, one – two. Release it, count, three – four.'

The way he lay, arms twisted. He was nearly in the position of swimming.

'Take a breath, one – two. Release it, count, three – four.'

Darling, little fish-bone. Show me you can breathe.

SIX

STRANGE, MY PARENTS were satisfied with their yellow lawn, their stained chairs. My little brother and I had a whole lake to play in but they remained there, by the house, lying like dead bodies on their broken loungers. Such a coupling of glamour and decay for children to come upon. There was mother's body, wet with oil, tanned in all her parts and an elegant thing laid out next to our poor father, crusted. He never could take the sun. It burned and burned him, but still his chair was pushed up beside hers; he had to be that close. Though she was shaded by dark glasses he was alert to her; in a shift of weight, a sigh, she could signify her needs. So they lay there. The glaring light, reflected in the windows of the house, shone down upon them both. 'A glass tan', my mother called it.

I didn't like to be there with them, kept my brother away too, when I could, for his innocence. No one should have witnessed the shameful way they were together, a woman keeping herself so private from the dry man always at her back. Later, when she'd had enough sun, my mother would rise, go into the house, and find some bed there to lie in. Sleep clung about her. As she silently moved through her day, from a bedroom to the lawn and back again, our father followed. Folding up the chairs behind, taking out the first glasses and lining them along the kitchen bench. As she slept he opened the small packets of mixed nuts and emptied them into bowls, took a cloth to the small tables, laid out fresh mats. He wore an apron for his work, then later wet down his hair and parted it along his pink scalp, put on a clean shirt. All the time waiting. All the time holding back, holding himself in for the minute when he was allowed to wake her, looking at his watch to check the exact minute when he could mix up the drink that she would sip while he sat on the bed beside her, carefully, like she was his own patient.

'It's six o'clock,' he said then. 'Time to think about getting up, Kate. Is there anything else you need?'

This was the time of day, when the sun was going down, that his wife wakened into the remaining light. She took a shower, changed into some lovely thing, some scarf, twisted into a thin bra top, some silk swathe flowing from a gold collar at her throat and her back left all bare. She might play with my little brother then, talk to us all like a mother.

'You're growing out of those jeans. You need a new pair', 'Remind me to make a shopping list', 'Did you have a nice time today?'

It was like she'd come back to us, putting cream on our father's sunburnt nose and his foolish smile when she did it. She showed me pictures of her favourite dresses in magazines, let me sit in her room while she put her make-up on.

'How do I look?'

'You're beautiful.'

I think we all seemed so happy then. My father said it, how it was our family's time of day, when anything could come true.

'Ask for anything you want,' he used to say, as he cracked ice into the drinks bucket; laid out barbeque meats on the grill. 'Anything, and you can have it too.'

'Can I have a glass of coke?'

'A kitten?'

'Disneyland?'

'Anything . . .' my father said. 'All you have to do is ask. Tell your mother, it could all come true.'

My mother, standing quietly among us, smiled. She stroked my hair.

'We'll have to get this cut,' she said. She fingered the strands. 'You probably think you're old enough for a hairstyle now.'

Perhaps we could have continued these scenes, the four of us, could have learned, with time, the trick that makes other families real. My father had had it with his own, a history, a set of customs to bear. How he must have longed, with his endless stories about the past, to continue a line, make good his promises. How he must have loved us to want to keep us in his eye.

'Please . . .'

Even now, through dreams, I hear the way he used to softly call for my mother in the night.

'Katherine. It's late . . .'

He used to wait up for her, long after the parties were over, the lights turned off and everyone gone home. Some slow ticking kept her awake and she used to roam the house at night, going from room to room, opening doors and cupboards, lingering in the hallway, in the dark.

'Please, Katherine . . .'

Even now, I hear him.

'Come to bed . . .'

How did it happen to him? That his life was left such a thin bit of cloth for him to twist? He waited nights for her, as well as the days. He took so many hours, so much sun for her pretty sake he was desiccated with waiting. All his young life gone. Of course my mother was a woman who could make addicts of even casual acquaintances, still . . . Even now I can't quite locate the precise nature of his need. Was it just a yearning for possession? A husband to a wife? That he wanted those primitive gifts from her, her beauty, cool distance? Or was it more, that he meant for them to occupy together the sad, cruel place where she lived, her unhappiness?

'What is it, darling? . . . Tell me what I can do.'

However it had happened – whether it was as simple as his own deep unknowing of her that, as always, bred the lust – his life was shrunk by now up onto dry land. My father wouldn't go fishing any more.

'Is there anything I can do to help?'

His lines were reeled in, the tackle stored. There would be no more cool water for his small boat.

'Please. Ask me anything . . .'

All of his hopes now gone into waiting.

When you learn to fish, it's on shore at first, putting the line high above you with one motion, letting it course behind you in a loop, catching it on the downturn and lifting it again so it rounds out in a grand arc before you. There is a memory I have of my father testing a new rod in this way, feeling the bend of the wood respond to his wrist, listening for the thin sound it makes as it whips back and forth through the fresh, wetted air. Later, waist-deep in waders in the river or fishing off the spit, the line is real. Every sweep of it conveys a fly to the water, the punctuation of the hook at the end of the trace gives the tiniest gesture weight. My father taught my mother the sense of what he already knew, the respect for materials, for silk line and split cane, the nylon trace fine as a hair. She learnt from him how to let the fly alight on the water, dance for a glint of a second on the skin of it, then be whisked off like flight. I think how the two of them used to take the boat out together, so early in the morning even my little brother and I were still sleeping . . . I imagine it. And together how they found that intimate thing, casting and drawing, casting and drawing, she letting her rod back while his was forward, he allowing her cast while his was drawn in.

They managed it then, I want to believe, a delicate interrogative, mostly unspoken. Instead of words only their thoughts looping through each other like the fine lines overhead, forming arcs, touching, releasing. There in silence was all my father's instruction: of cast and drift and the scent of the air, of delicate currents. In silence was the thinness, newness of their feelings, like the untempered water all around them. I imagine my father out there on the lake with his wife, examining the fly at the end of her line for faults if the day had been slow, taking his little scissors from the tackle box and cutting it loose, changing it for another. I know he had one he called Phelon's Favourite, for so many years he used it. I once watched him tie it from a fragment of feather, a tiny strand of gold to mark an insect's head.

How easy, change. These things happened so long ago and my father, my mother ... Now you would not guess the way they used to be together. Yet strange, they did seem satisfied with what was left. Dry summers on the lawn, a house fit only for parties. In the way he maintained his attention to her my mother was right. *Your father will always be My Boyfriend.*

There he stood now, at the bar, at the table. Every surface was immaculate.

'See what your mother wants, Janey. Ask if there's anything we can fix her ...'

Jim Little was running around in circles, around and around the sofa and jumping over it.

'Can I have an aeroplane? A rabbit?'

'Anything,' my father said. 'You can have anything you want.' He picked up Jim Little and swung him in the air.

74

'Can I have a Superman costume? With a cape that flies?'

'Anything.'

Our mother stood at the window looking out across the lake. Her dark-blue and pink dress was hanging open at the back so we could see, anybody could see, the deep line of her shoulders and her smooth tan.

I heard her ask, 'Can someone get me a cigarette?'

Jim Little was dancing around my father, his voice getting louder and louder.

'A cape that flies. A cape that flies,' he was chanting, and my father kept saying 'Anything! Anything!' and pretending to catch him.

'I said, can someone get me – '

Suddenly everything was quiet. My father scrabbled for the Rothmans on the bar. I saw how his fingers dug into the packet to take one out.

'Quick,' he said to me. 'Give it to your mother. Be that little waitress, honey.'

This was how it worked between the two of them now. My mother giving just enough instruction to keep my father at her hem, and she in turn used to his attentions. So practised were their mannerisms, their friendly operations together, they may not even have needed two children to prove marriage. But there we were: twelve years old, five years old. Together we represented what was unfinished. I lit a match, held it to the tip and sucked in like I knew how to. When the end caught I took the cigarette over to my mother, along with her drink, six ice cubes, as she liked it.

'Room Service,' I said.

She should have known all the time; my father should have known: Children have it in them to bring the ending down. Perhaps in pieces, a bank crumbling, the look in a parent's eye, or all at once, the land unjointed and a gap left where grass used to grow roots.

The day it began for our family it was quiet, so gentle. The sky was soft as a goose's belly. I was taking my little brother to the river. We were down on the second beach, past Cady's, last house on the point, and nothing ahead of us but a long sheet of sand. We were the only two people on the beach and for a while my little brother walked slowly with me, telling me some long story about shipwrecks, pirates, all stuff he'd got out of *Peter Pan*, all the children escaping.

'I love that boy,' he kept saying. 'I like him best. More than the others and that dog.'

The water slopped, opaque, at our feet and his voice ran on with ideas and stories. He said he wanted to play Peter and I'd be the rest of the children, taking them in turns. There was a plan that at the river we'd discover Captain Hook but he'd be nice to us this time, he'd let us go on his boat.

'I'm going to go on up ahead and arrange it,' he said. 'You can swim to meet me at the river. It's part of the game.'

I never worried about him playing on his own, often it was what he wanted. After he was gone I waded into the water. It was warm, even when I was waist-deep, and I sunk down into it and pushed off underwater, one slow glide. The river wasn't so far this way, and as I came up for air and started towards it, arm over, ear flat on the water, I felt already in my first few strokes, mouth open, that I could taste the water changing. Taste the sweet green of the river channel flowing into the lake.

Take a breath – one, two.

Long gliding strokes.

How pleased my father would be, I was thinking, if he could see the swimmer he'd made me. All the years of lessons had left me so strong. I swam evenly this way for half a mile or so, then flipped over on to my back and turned into the water again in a half dive. The lake seemed dark and private as I forged my way into it but lightened as I started to rise, creaming into bubbles as I broke the surface.

Take a breath – one, two.

The air was warm on my face, soft.

Long gliding strokes.

I swam all the way down to where the beach curved and the sand rose in a bar. I stood up then. The lake thinned into shallows at this part and it was easier to walk. All around me there was silence, the pale sky empty and the beach deserted. I walked through the shallows for a while, kicking the water in front of me, then turned up on to dry beach. A man was watching me.

'Hello.'

He was my mother's friend.

He said he'd been watching me swim, that he'd been watching me for a long time. It seemed very calm. He smoked for a while, looking out across the lake. He put his hand out to detain me when I thought I heard my brother's cry, the smoke from his cigarette rising from his mouth, his fingers. When he kissed me I could taste the smoke and that's how it started. Not there on the beach. In the bush, he said. He knew a place where we could go.

I think that was the day I first began to understand my father's lost instinct for the water. The light insect sound of the silk line, my swimming lessons at the Institute . . . All these things, acts of the body that he thought would protect us, give identity . . . Really, they were a disguise for forgetting. Although in later years I taunted myself that I was the one in our family who had to change things, that it was my role to cast the first sin. I know now the falling away, the darkness of our summers had started years ago and it was nobody's guilt.

'Come closer, honey . . . I've been waiting so long for you.'

Things just happen, that's all. And then they're gone.

After my father became used to taking my mother out, listening for her line to catch and not his own, he couldn't do it on his own again. The fishing had changed for him. All his years of solitude before, casting, drawing in; the memories of times on the lake with his father; threading the trace through the fly's eyelet when the other, trembling, couldn't do it; being alert to the shift of movement in the boat, the drift of it . . . All this finished for him and he became the person who was left. Dried out, only words for stories.

Jim Little never even noticed I'd been away. Afterwards, I ran so fast to the river where he was playing near the boats and, though I felt I'd been gone such a long time it was like time in fairy stories; hours it seemed, but really you could count off those forlorn acts in minutes. Jimmy was still busy arranging the plates of leaves that indicated our home, showing me where the front door was, the window through which Peter would come and make his nightly visit. He'd marked out with stones the borders between one place ending and another beginning.

'Can we start the game now? Are you ready?'

For the first time I looked down at my brother but I couldn't see his face.

'Janey . . .'

All I could see were the thick walls of bush in the place where Cady had taken me, the heaped, packed earth for me to lie on.

'Don't you love me?'

There were leaves, the glint of sun through their dark oval shapes, and the heat of him, and all his prying words.

'Come closer, honey. Don't be shy.'

He broke branches to make space for us.

'That's better . . . That's nice . . .'

There was the sudden green smell of split bark.

Now, going back over these events, I think my mother knew it all. Sitting at her dressing-table that night, somewhere under her smooth expression she knew it. That I would take her limbs, her hair. That some day I would become her, smooth with cosmetics and calm to the mirror's surface, all the time carrying hooks in my pockets for men.

'How do I look?'

'You're beautiful.'

She'd let me sit on the end of the bed while she put her make-up on. Her face was tilted to the glass, the planes and shapings of it, brow and cheek and chin.

'Boys, boys, boys . . .'

She drew around the edge of her mouth and filled in the space with pale colour, pressing her lips together so they were perfectly covered. 'When you're least expecting, there's one at your back . . .' She kissed herself in the mirror then drew back, looked deep into the glass, deep into her own lovely face.

'One day I dread you'll tell me you're in love.' She spun around on her stool, rose, all of a piece, upon her high thin shoes. 'But forget about you. Where's that baby? I want to put him in a bath and clean him myself. Jim Little?' she called, and she was out of the room, her scent left behind.

After she had gone I went over to where she had been sitting. Scent bottle, lipstick furled from its gold tube like a little tongue . . . All her things were laid out there before the mirror. I touched them, the thick creams in jars, tissues blotted red with colour. I unstopped the bottle of her fragrance and the sharp, sweet smell came up at me again, adult.

'Come here, honey . . .'

Her things were warm to the touch. The creams, the lotions. I could spread them on my own skin.

'Don't be shy . . .'

It was just once at first, letting myself be taken, then more times, over and over until it was me myself going back for more. Leaving my family, leaving my little brother playing while the tides in the river were rising.

Still, it was the lovely time of the day, the summer-house was so light then. I left my mother's room and went out to where they all were. Mother. Father. Little brother. The curtains were open to the last of the golden light and the benches and tables were clean, stripped of food ends and the bottles laid up shining along the bar.

'Can I have a peanut, Daddy?'

Jim Little was dancing at my father's feet as he mixed drinks.

'Can I have a glass of lemonade?'

Soon visitors would be here, the cards were laid out already on their special table, but right now it was just the four of us alone together. Jim Little's skin was sweet and shining from his bath and I had a towel open for him. I wrapped it around his frail body tightly like a bandage.

'I love you. I love you.'

My father passed a glass to my mother and she took it from him, smiling, and light held us, just then it held us in gold.

'You can have anything you want,' Daddy said.

And for those last few minutes while the sun still lit the room, before darkness came, I believed. Ice shifted in the glasses. Our family. For minutes, seconds, we were held in light.

SEVEN

YOUR BLOOD IS full of air, your body is. This is something you should know when treating your patient. Don't let the other things sicken you, the slimy touch of skin, the piece of weed extending like silk from the nostril. Get on with your job. You know what to do.

Before beginning any form of artificial respiration it's necessary that you first make sure you can hear no breathing. Lay your ear close to the open mouth, look deep inside it. Remember, at this point you may feel no pulse, at neck or wrist there may be no signs of life, but this is not to say the patient is dead. Even doctors sometimes have to hold a tiny mirror, a glass, above the lips to be sure. If you are outdoors it is unlikely you will have accessories like these; you must rely instead on your own senses. Is the chest moving, even slightly? When you bend over the face, can you feel the lightest breath against your cheek?

If there really is no air at all you must act quickly. You have no idea how long this body has been unconscious; even if you took him from the water just seconds ago it takes only a very few minutes for the brain tissues, deprived of blood flow and oxygen, to die. After that the nerve control that keeps the body alive will fail. Strong swimmers, of course, who have rescued in the water, are able to give mouth-to-mouth resuscitation between strokes, so lessening the possibility of unconsciousness once the victim is on the beach. The reality of enacting this life-saving procedure, however, is more than difficult. Panic, fearfulness, the instinct to put speed above all other priorities in getting the body to dry land . . . These factors will tend to overwhelm. Even the most experienced swimmer could find that he or she is actually pushing the head of the victim under the water as she swims. Afterwards, that person may imagine the victim gasping, mouth wide open, attempting air, before being submerged again and again in the waves. More likely it was the swimmer's own breath that was heard.

Despite this, and irrespective of whether or not this kind of rescue has been attempted, the first thing to do on shore is to get the patient on his back. If there are obstructions in the mouth, clear them. Do this by scooping with two curved fingers, reaching as deeply into the cavity as is possible to remove debris, blood, vomit, mud. Additional matter lodged far back in the gullet can be removed by the forefinger alone using a hooking action to 'flick' back hard objects: small pebbles, for example, shells, a plug of sand.

As soon as the mouth is clean you can proceed.

Bend the head right back so the tongue cannot block the air passages and cause choking and suffocation. There are several ways of doing this. The safest is to press the head with the heel of your hand resting on the forehead and your fingers on the bridge of the nose. Alternatively, you can adjust the neck by placing a hand beneath it and lifting it upwards. The set of the body, once out of the water, will tell you whether or not you should adopt this handling position. Is there an unusual diplacement of limbs, for example? A twist to the pelvis? Is the neck turned at an unnatural angle? Any of these would indicate that there has been severe battery in the water and so alert you to potentially serious damage to the spine. Be so careful. Make sure the neck is well aligned by the pressure of your own hand but do not attempt under any circumstance to rearrange the arms, the legs. Your patient is not sleeping – and besides, there is no time now to make him lovely.

Once the throat is extended, the head back, the airway is then clear to breathe. Occasionally spontaneous inhalation will begin at this point, the patient reviving in a matter of seconds. If this is not the case, immediately commence artificial respiration as detailed below.

At the softest lower part, around the tiny openings of the nostrils, pinch the nose shut. Use the same hand you have pushing down on the forehead to do this, with your other hand pull the jaw open as wide as possible. Of course, when the muscles are limp and the head thrown back the mouth will fall open naturally, but the extra hold you have on the jaw, your fingers tight around the chin, will act, slightly, as a vice. Know this as a safety precaution. Should there be involuntary spasms of the body, the head is kept safe. Even so, take care as you grip the chin that your fingers do not interfere with the mouth. You need it clear for the next step.

If, during all this time, you are alone, and while you are handling the body in this way, you may wish to shout for help. It's your instinct, a thin thing, and of no use. If the beach is empty calling is hopeless, you know it. Though it may seem that hours are passing by, really these are minutes, seconds. That drip from a strand of your hair falling onto the forehead of your patient, that's real time. In the lifeblood of anatomy it's eternity. Your shouts, calls, if the day is misty and there is no one about, are in vain. Emotion cannot dictate action now. It's what you do that brings life, not words.

Concentrating then fully on the task at hand you may use your thumb to bring the patient's head up to increase the air passage even further – but don't let your hand press on the base of the throat. This is the windpipe, and a delicate organ for bruising and damage. Think of it as a soft reed, an instrument. Any pressure on this young part will stop off all breathing and, with the victim already in a state of deep unconsciousness, it is doubtful you would even notice. Therefore keep the area quite free, open to the air. Let the light play across it. For a minute see the whole body, the form of it, resting weightless on the curved sand.

Now you have him.

Inhale deeply then and seal your mouth around the patient's open mouth. Can you feel your lips pressing as if on a cold wound? Can you be sure no air can escape around your lips, are they widely apart, fully covering

86

the opening? Blow then, but gently, be gentle with him, blow into his mouth.

'Aaaah . . .'

There is your sigh, your old life, sounding in his cave.

'Aaaah . . .'

Fill his lungs with your sighing, your expiration. Make your own inhalation as rich, as deep as possible. Do it.

'Aaaah . . .'

Again.

'Aaah . . .'

As you do it, as you breathe into him, his chest will expand and then you must immediately take your mouth off his so his lungs may expel the air that you have breathed into them. Is this clear? Are you understanding? Four deep breaths into the mouth, the chest filling, then expiring, filling, then expiring. No matter what your thoughts are at this time, the sequence of your actions is vital. Count, one – two. Count, three – four. Don't let yourself be persuaded to hurry, nor should you linger. These first four breaths you give him are so important, don't wait for the full flattening of the chest between each. Oxygen is vital now, you have to get as much oxygen as you can into the lungs. Don't be afraid to blow as deeply as you can; the air you breathe into him is from your mouth and windpipe only, there are no poisons in it. The small amount of carbon dioxide from your lungs is too small to be toxic. You can't harm him further. You can't, with your breath, do damage. You're giving him oxygen, keep remembering that. Oxygen for his blood, his watery heart. Oxygen for his brain, the tiny nerve ends wavering like anemone. Oxygen for his eyes, feet, hands. Oxygen for his whole body running lightly, a wisp.

'Don't leave me!'

There was a glint on the water, a call in thin air. Don't think about that.

'Help me!'

Don't. It's too late. You can't hasten him into life with your panic, concentrate on what you're doing. All of it, each crumb of a second of it.

Breathe in, one – two.

Breathe out, three – four.

Breathe in, one – two.

Breathe out, three – four.

This is real. Put your finger at the pulse of his neck. Can you feel it? That little beating sac, bird's heart? Is it alive?

Certainly if, during these first four communications with the patient, matter rises in the mouth as you breathe into it, a recovery is more than likely. Breathing has started and now the channels are sluicing themselves, readying the passage for regular inhalation and expiration. Simply sweep out the contents of the mouth using your fingers in the method described earlier, remembering to place the head on one side so the liquids can drain. You're one of the lucky ones. Others, facing no such signs of life, must immediately commence the next phase of recovery.

External chest compression can be seen as a violent act, instigating the circulation of the blood by making the heart pump artificially. To make the compression you will be depressing the breastbone onto the heart that lies behind it, forcing the blood out of it and into the arteries. When the pressure is released the heart can fill up again from the same veins. To perform this on a child is not easy. Applying such weight to a smaller torso can easily cause damage to the ribs and internal organs, and for this reason, for the reason of a framework of bone and muscle that is softer than yours, there must be some alteration of technique if you are not to cause rupture and bleeding. Therefore you will be using one hand to make the compression instead of the usual two-handed method applied to most adults.

First, make sure the patient is on a hard surface – so as to provide support at the back for the moment when you come down hard upon the chest. Then feel quickly along the breastbone for the exact point on which to apply pressure. If you imagine the length of the ladder of bones as being divided into three sections, the part you need to find is two-thirds down, where the second and third sections meet. The child is thin so you will have no problem locating the relevant part of bone: you can see it articulated there beneath the whitened skin on the chest. Put the heel of one hand on the point there and, keeping your arms perfectly straight, lean forward, push into him, using the weight of your whole body for pressure.

Don't bang or thump the bone. The anatomy of a child will be traumatized enough by the sheer weight of your body leaning upon it. Don't you think you're doing enough? Were the situation, in this instance, less grave you would not even contemplate compression. The body is too small. As soon as you have come down on it release your weight. Immediately drop back, still kneeling. Leave your hands in position. Now you will see the breastbone rise, and for a split second will believe the cold boy is breathing. Once he appears to have air in him, lean down again and press upon his chest as before, as if you were forcing all the breath out of him once more.

For someone acting alone, this is not easy. You must work more swiftly on a child than on an adult, continuing with artificial respiration as you do so. Start off by making the compressions at the usual rate of eighty per minute but quickly increase this to 100 per minute. After the first fifteen compressions give two full mouth-to-mouth ventilations, follow this with a further fifteen chest compressions, two mouth-to-mouth ventilations ... and so on, in sequence, quickly, regularly. Keep going, don't stop, keep pressing, keep breathing. Fifteen compressions, two ventilations, fifteen compressions, two ventilations. Keep going, keep going. Where is your time now? There is no time.

Whatever is happening around you, don't stop. A crowd may have gathered at your back, there's disturbance in the air, perhaps they're talking to you – don't hear them. You're trying to get the heart beating, the chest breathing spontaneously again. Keep checking for a pulse. You've already felt at the neck after the first four ventilations, if there is nothing there, if, as doctors say 'the pulse is absent', keep on with the chest compressions. One minute later feel again, feel for the lightest beat of blood through the artery there, it could start any minute, and if there's nothing check again and keep checking, every three minutes from now on, press the shallow dent on the throat with your finger, any minute now, any minute. If the heart has begun to beat, if for a fraction you hear it, or if there is a pulsation in the neck artery, stop the compressions immediately. It would be dangerous to continue pumping the heart artificially when it has already found its own natural rhythm. Put your finger there again, did you only imagine you felt it jump? Whatever happens, whatever you pretend, don't stop breathing air into him. You know a heart can beat for a few seconds, a pulse quicken, but without an involuntary intake of breath it's only a phantom coming alive. Breath, that's what you're waiting for, the first harsh gasp for air. That's your sign, that's what your own heart is racing for. Air for him. Air in his body. A disgorge of water from the mouth and air to breathe, cloud, light.

What do I need you to know now? How long to continue? You know the answer already; people don't stop this thing. After minutes even the panic is gone and what is left to you is process: the eye on the second hand, the finger at the throat. It's process, it's what you're doing to him now. Compressions, counting, your mouth on his mouth, your hand on his head . . . It's process, process. You don't stop this thing. Even after the others have come and pulled you off him, still you don't want to stop it. He's yours. You took him from the water. You know what to do. You've been with him there all along, before someone on a boat saw you, before people came. Before they called the doctor, before, you alone were all his company. You were the one natural with the body, all the time it was you. Your lips around his cold lips, your hands around his wet head. He was yours. All the time you knew what to do.

Water rescue manuals and first aid books claim grand successes, line drawings show it: Grown men and women propped up like happy dolls, contented recovery positions from now on. In theory the aim is to continue with resuscitation until the patient is breathing normally again – perhaps after several hours of both mouth-to-mouth ventilation, external chest compression and a combination of the two.

'Carry on without interruption and use any bystanders to send urgent messages for aid and an ambulance.'

In the picture it arrives, inside, two friendly men with blankets.

'Loosen any tight clothes that may be constricting the patient, keep him warm . . .'

'At this point, if it is to hand, a little brandy can be of use . . .'

You'll turn pages and pages of recoveries before they tell you the truth about time. Continue, continue. That's how it starts. Any minute now, the pulse will catch, a breath, you'll hear it. Continue, you can cheat on time, aren't all book deaths just pretend? Continue, and you turn the page again.

'Continue until you are prevented from doing so by a

doctor or someone experienced or in authority', that's what the book says now. 'Even when all the correct techniques have been applied . . . Even when compression appears to have had some success . . .'

You turn the page.

'Many patients whose heartbeat and respiration stop can never recover . . .'

You turn, you turn.

'. . . At the onset of the incident this cannot be foretold.'

Come away now. Leave it.

'Even when . . .'

'Even when . . .'

Leave it. There's nothing you can do. You know at the lake there was always too much water.

Even in dry summer, water. That part of the country was a carved-out bowl for rivers running to it, rain. My father could predict the floods and freak storms in their thick cloud colours, yellow for thunder, indigo for lightning. It was geography, he said, the cold plunging depth of a volcanic lake and the warm air banked up around the mountains. Marriage in the way they attracted, in the way water banked up and had to break. We swam in water that changed colour by the weather. See-through for the hot days in the shallows, pale chiffon-blue deeper, dark underskirts beneath. Other times, when close storms held the lake still as black glass, you could believe it might bruise you . . . Then the wind blew up and the whole surface shattered and cut into a million shining bits, exposing the jelly insides of the water within, cobalt, silken.

So much water. Miles of it under you, washing through underwater caves, one shelf of water tipping over into another, vast secret lakes, a whole world of water beneath, prehistoric. It was hundreds of miles of past and future washing through itself in endless, moonless tides. Water, water, all water. Of course our mark upon it, our frail kicking ... Of course it could have been no more than leaves scattered across the surface. So much water, you can't change it. You can imagine other things you could have done, if you want, rack over in your mind details, events, names of people and their ages ... But does any of this give you more than what you started out with?

The water has them, those people you pretend were your life. It has you. It's water's pulse beating in your wrist now. You know it too. The lake, she's your lovely body now, with all her openings. Close your eyes, she's still there. Some days the surface of water is pulled over like satin, others it's rumpled and bony. There's your memory. Pure images of tide and depth and the colour of the water ... These are things you can still use. Who you were, who you are now, your people ... They're drowned in her. All the rest is water.

I remember how, long ago, my little brother and I used to go out into the summer rain. We were disappearing or returning, I don't know. We were going into water. There at the lake, rain was so gentle. It was a drift, a veil of grey and silver, like the sails of ghost ships, gauzy. There was cloud in the rain too, white mists lifting off the lake so water tended into the air like it lived there. Slowly it stained, there was no violence to it, no individual drops, it was melting rain. The beach sunk into a deeper colour, and it happened so gradually that at first you could see no change at all. Then you would press on the sand with your toes and find it warm, slaty. The powder of it had condensed with moisture, you could squeeze it, shape it into castles and islands and towers. Whole cities we could leave moulded on the beach and all the time as we worked the rain softened them, merged into vague dream shapes, hills.

Up behind the beach rain smoothed the dry grass down and the fields of lupins were shiny, their yellow like wet paint against the pale grey.

In rain we could take off our clothes and walk down the beach and into the lake in one continuous gliding movement. There was no telling where land ended, waves began. Sand and water dissolved into each other, blotted in mist. Nothing else existed on those days except two children. Watch them. Two with the whole beach to themselves, the whiteness of cloud and water swirling at their feet as they dance, round and around, round and around . . . With each turn becoming smaller, further away, smaller and smaller in the distance until you can't see them at all.